THE THIEF OF WORLDS

Favorites by Bruce Coville

The Enchanted Files

Cursed

Hatched

Trolled

Aliens Ate My Homework

Always October

The Dragonslayers

The Ghost in the Third Row

Goblins in the Castle

I Left My Sneakers in Dimension X

Into the Land of the Unicorns

I Was a Sixth Grade Alien

Jeremy Thatcher, Dragon Hatcher

The Monsters of Morley Manor

The Monster's Ring

My Teacher Is an Alien

The Prince of Butterflies

And Dozens More!

THE THIEF OF WORLDS

BRUCE COVILLE

RANDOM HOUSE NEW YORK

For my first mentor, Helen Buckley Simkewicz,
who managed to get a full draft out of me nearly fifty years ago

. . . and for my editor, Mallory Loehr,
without whom I never would have brought it over the finish line.

Text copyright © 2021 by Bruce Coville
Jacket art copyright © 2021 by Matt Rockefeller

All rights reserved. Published in the United States by Random House
Children's Books, a division of Penguin Random House LLC, New York.

Random House and the colophon are registered trademarks
of Penguin Random House LLC.

Visit us on the Web! rhcbooks.com

Educators and librarians, for a variety of teaching tools,
visit us at RHTeachersLibrarians.com

Library of Congress Cataloging-in-Publication Data
Names: Coville, Bruce, author.
Title: The thief of worlds / Bruce Coville.
Description: First edition. | New York : Random House, [2021] |
Audience: Ages 8–12.
Summary: To save heavily polluted Earth and his ailing mother, eleven-year-old
Hurricane must travel to magical worlds, aboard a giant, winged tiger, to rescue the wind
and other elements.
Identifiers: LCCN 2020023012 | ISBN 978-0-385-39251-8 (hardcover) |
ISBN 978-0-385-39252-5 (library binding) |
ISBN 978-0-385-39253-2 (ebook)
Subjects: CYAC: Fantasy. | Winds—Fiction. | Magic—Fiction.
Classification: LCC PZ7.C8344 Th 2021 | DDC [Fic]—dc23

The text of this book is set in 12.25-point Adobe Caslon Pro.
Interior design by Jen Valero

Printed in the United States of America
10 9 8 7 6 5 4 3 2 1
First Edition

Forget not that the earth delights to feel your bare feet
and the winds long to play with your hair.

—KHALIL GIBRAN

CONTENTS

PART THREE: WHAT DREAMS MAY COME

part one

WINDLESS

MY STRANGE BIRTH

The wind had stopped. Just stopped, as if someone had killed it.

Which meant that I was miserable.

Yeah, I know. *Everyone* in Chicago was miserable. And not only Chicago. The wind had stopped all across the world! For the first couple of days scientists had thought it was some weird coincidence. Now they were starting to freak out.

I was already freaking out. For me, losing the wind was like losing a best friend.

See, I've always had a thing for the wind. The people around me knew it. Back when Mom and Gran and I lived in Mississippi, the neighbors called me Breezeboy and laughed about how I danced with the wind. What they didn't know was that the wind was talking to me. Okay, I could never really understand it. But I always felt it was simply a matter of time before somehow, some way, I would be able to.

Mom has a dish towel printed with the blessing MAY THE WIND BE ALWAYS AT YOUR BACK, and for me that has almost always been true. When I was little, if I went outside, the wind would dance around my feet, then push me gently from behind as if it was playing with me. We even had a game, the wind and me. I would toss my hat in the air, and the wind would swirl it away . . . then carry it back and drop it onto my head. Once the wind even protected me from some bullies, rising from nowhere and blowing dirt into their eyes when they were about to pound me.

At least, I thought all that had happened. But that was when I was a little kid, so it was hard to be sure. By the time Mom and I moved to Chicago, after Dad was killed by that drunk driver, I had stopped thinking the wind was trying to tell me secrets. But my longing for it, my *need* for it, never ceased. Now that it was gone I was afraid I might go crazy.

On the third day with no wind Mom and I were in our apartment on the fourth floor of the Jerrold Arms. That name makes the place sound pretty classy, and maybe it had been when it was built about a billion years ago. Now . . . well, now it's pretty run-down. Actually, "run-down" is too kind. Truth is, it's kind of a dump.

It was early evening and it was hot. I glanced beyond Mom to our curtains. They hung limp and unmoving. God, how I wanted the wind to blow!

Mom was in her old red chair, mending a torn pair of jeans. The chair had been mended, too, since Mom had rewoven the places where the fabric had worn thin. "Too much throwing away, not enough fixing" was her take on the world. She was all about fixing stuff.

I was sprawled on the floor beside her, trying to draw. I was also complaining about the heat and the lack of wind. It wouldn't have been so bad if we'd had AC, but we were way too broke for that.

"You should go outside," Mom told me.

Without looking up, I said, "I could just crawl into the oven. It would be about as comfortable." I didn't look up because I was staring with annoyance at the spot where some sweat had dropped from my forehead onto the picture I was working on. I draw a lot, mostly fantasy creatures. Griffins are my favorites. I love their odd mixture of parts.

"The oven would be cramped," Mom said. "Outside is bigger."

She started to say something else but coughed instead, coughed that raspy cough that scared me. I jumped up to fetch her a glass of water. She took a few sips, breathing a little more deeply after each of them. When the coughing spell ended, I dropped back to the floor.

"Tell me the story," I said.

"Aren't you afraid you'll wear it out?"

"Nah, it gets better every time you tell it. Besides, it's

about wind, so this would be a good night for it, since there isn't any outside!"

She made a little snort. "It's not just about wind, it's about you. Maybe you should listen to other people's stories now and then."

As things turned out, I would be doing a lot of that before this was all over. But I didn't know that then. All I said was "That's why I like this one—I'm the only one who has it! Besides, you tell it good!"

"Tell it *well*, flatterer."

I rolled my eyes. "If we can't have wind, we can at least have a story about it."

Mom picked up her mending and sighed. "Let me think for a minute."

That meant yes. All I had to do was wait.

Sounds from the street filtered through our open window: a car alarm set off by some idiot; a girl blasting her boyfriend for being late; Herbie across the street practicing his drums like we weren't all just about suffocating.

Mom began to cough again. The sound started in her throat, then spread until her entire body shook with spasms. The cough was already stronger than she was and getting worse each day that the air lay stagnant and still over the city. She leaned back and closed her eyes, her face pinched with the effort of trying to hide the pain. Her slender fingers trembled on the faded red arm of the chair. I reached up to put my hand on hers.

"How about that story?" she whispered.

"How about you just go to bed," I replied.

She bopped me with the shirt she had been mending. "Who's the mother here? *I* send *you* to bed, remember? And it's too early for that. So zip your lips and listen."

I smiled. "If you insist, Mother."

"Hush," she said, and gave my nose a tweak. Even though I had turned eleven back in May, she still liked to do that.

After the tweak she was silent for a moment. I closed my eyes, getting ready to listen. I had been practicing seeing the story in my head, trying to make it as real as possible, filling in new details every time I heard it.

Mom's voice, soft but strong, led me into the picture.

It was back when we were living in Mississippi. We knew there was a storm coming, and your gran said it was going to be a bad one. Your gran had a way about that, about storms. She'd been watching the signs and getting more fretful every day. She had reason to worry, what with me pregnant, your daddy off to the war, and no one in town—which, I have to admit, was a few miles away—who much cared what might happen to us. Oh, that town! Never saw such people for minding their own business unless they thought there was a cent

to be had in someone else's. Dang pennygrinders knew there wasn't any money to be had at our place, so they pretty much left us alone.

Wouldn't have been so bad if the house wasn't in such rough shape. But it was all we had, and your gran and I were glad enough of it.

It was Thursday, late summer. I was outside, taking clothes off the line, trying to get them down before the storm hit. The wind was high, and the clothes were whipping and whirling so much I was afraid I was gonna lose half of them before I could get back inside. So there I was, near to busting with holding you inside me, the wind wrapping the sheets around me so that I looked like a big white beach ball, when your gran comes running out and shouts, "Get in the house right now, Jessie! Leave the rest of the clothes! Ain't safe out here. Storm's getting close and we got to get settled!"

We had boarded up the windows the day before. Now we braced the doors with planks.

Lord, how that wind did blow! I heard it rise, and something inside me told me it was gonna be as bad as your gran said. Wasn't long before it was howling around that old house, shaking the walls and making the timbers creak.

As if all that wasn't enough, you decided that was a good time to be a-borning!

Your gran hustled me down the stairs to the cellar. Nearest hospital was forty miles away, and we didn't have a car. But your gran had been bringing babies into the world a long time before I ever thought of having you. We took our lanterns and some food and some water down with us. Momma told me to sit tight while she went back upstairs to drag a mattress off one of the beds. She hauled it down the steps and pulled it into a corner. Then she made me lie down and told me to breathe real deep.

And all the while she was doing this, the storm was tearing at the house like a pack of wildcats screaming to get at us.

Things kept getting worse. You got more and more interested in being born, and that storm got more and more interested in blowing our house clean away. Me, I was lying there yelling and hollering, with your poor gramma washing my face and telling me, "Push, darlin'! Push to get that baby out!"

And still that storm kept getting bigger and louder.

Then the rain started. Honest to heaven, child, I doubt it bucketed down any harder the day Noah closed the doors on the Ark. And still the wind shrieked around the house as if some-one was being killed right outside our window. Then the wind busted through . . . blew the boards right off one of those little cellar windows and sent glass flying all over the place!

And with all that going on, every minute you were getting closer and closer to being born.

The house started to shake. I could feel it shudder on its foundation as the wind smashed against it. We heard a ter-rible howl, like Lucifer falling from heaven, then a cracking sound, and then the house was gone. Gone! The wind ripped it right from over top of us, splitting it into boards and shingles and broken glass. The whole thing blew away like it was scraps of paper.

And that was the very moment you made your entrance!

So there we were, the three of us in that tiny cellar. The rain was pouring in. I was screaming because I thought I was going to die before I even got to know you, you were squalling because that's what babies do, and your gran was trying to quiet both of us. Finally she snatched you up, leaned over you to protect you from the rain, and started yelling, "Help! Help!"

Shouting for help in the middle of that storm seemed pretty dang foolish to me. Except help came! I don't know from where. I don't know how. I don't even know what it was. All I know is that even though the storm was still raging, suddenly the wind and rain were gone from the cellar. I saw a huge winged shape above us. And it wasn't moving! Wind that could blow away a house whipped around it, and this thing just hung in the sky without moving!

Then a soft voice, a voice I could hear even with that wind screeching like a band of demons, whispered, "Rest. Sleep. You and yours are safe."

The last thing I remember was two golden eyes staring down at me from the storm. Then I fell asleep. Asleep! How can a person fall asleep when there's no roof, and a raging storm, and a brand-new baby, and something that shouldn't even be up in the sky?

Your gran told me later that when she covered you up and laid you down beside me, a breeze danced around your head, tugging at the corners of the blanket. She said you looked happy *and peaceful. So she kissed you, then named you, and that was the last thing she remembered from that night.*

"And that's why I love the wind so much!" I crowed.

"That's why, Hurricane," Mom answered. "That's why, my hurricane boy."

ZEPHRON

Two days later Chicago had moved from edginess to the border of panic. That's not me talking. It's what all the radio stations were saying. Not surprisingly, the internet chatter, which I kept checking at the library, was utterly bonkers.

It wasn't just Chi-town, of course. People all over the world were flat-out terrified.

As for me, it was all made worse by the fact that Mom was getting sicker. She wasn't able to get up at all now, so I stayed beside her bed to keep her company. I'm not sure that did any good. She could tell how upset I was, the way moms always can. Thing was, I knew it was only going to get worse. Despite the emergency restrictions on cars and trucks that the mayor had slapped down, with no wind to blow away the pollution Chicago's air was getting filthier by the hour.

I did what I could to keep the apartment cool. But what I could wasn't much—basically I kept a big bowl of ice cubes in Mom's room, with a fan blowing across it. The fan's speed went up and down because the city was having brownouts, since everyone who did have AC was using it full-time on high.

I was sick, too. Not sick like Mom and the others who were having trouble breathing. I was sick with fear for my mother. I was also sick in my soul. The wind had been my special friend since that crazy night when I was born. Now it had been snatched away without warning, without any way of knowing why or how.

Late that afternoon Mom reached up, took my hand, and said, "Hurricane, look at me."

Her voice was ragged. I tried to hide how much it scared me.

"Listen to your momma," she went on. "Stop worrying. There's nothing you can do about this. Soon enough the wind will start up again. The bad air will blow away, and we'll both feel—"

She was interrupted by the cough. She spit some blood into a tissue, then went on as if nothing had happened. "You'll feel better. The city will calm down. Everything will be all right. So you should stop worrying."

"And you should stop talking! It makes your cough worse."

She sighed and turned her head away.

"Do you want some tea with lemon and honey?" I asked, desperate to do something, *anything*, to make her feel better.

She started to answer, then closed her mouth and simply nodded.

"Good job not talking!" I said.

I was rewarded with a smile.

I left her side and began rattling around in our tiny kitchen. Despite the heat, I put water on to boil, then washed a cup. It was old and had a crack in one side, but the crimson rose painted on the front made it Mom's favorite. That done, I went to look out the window. I quickly turned away, not wanting to see the yellowish haze that covered the city.

When the kettle whistled I put a tea bag in the cup, then tipped the kettle over it. A small cloud of steam rose as the scalding water poured down. I let the tea steep for a minute, then carried the cup back to my mother.

She was asleep. I set the cup on the nightstand and whispered, "Mom?"

She didn't answer.

I took her hand, pressed it, then shook her shoulder.

Nothing.

I shook her harder but got no reaction. What should I do? We had no phone—our service had been turned off the month before. I didn't want to leave Mom, but since Martha-across-the-hall was at work, the only way to get help was to go for it myself.

I put my head against Mom's chest. She was breathing, but it was *so* shallow! I shook her again. No response at all. I bolted from the apartment and raced down four flights of stairs, then out into the windless street. The heat hit me like a wall. I ignored it and headed for the clinic ten blocks to the north.

The streets were fairly empty. No surprise . . . no one wanted to be out in this stuff if they could avoid it. Running through the gritty air made me cough almost as hard as my mother had. By the time I burst into the clinic to give a nurse my story, I was gasping and sobbing.

The clinic was crowded. Even so, two hours later they had managed to get Mom into one of the few remaining beds. The room was small, so I stood in the hall to wait as the doctor examined her. After several minutes he stepped out. My gut knotted when I saw the look on his face.

"Is she going to be okay?" I whispered.

He hesitated, then said, "If the air clears up she should be fine."

"That's a pretty big if."

The doctor sighed. "The air conditioning here is old and can't keep up. I would send your mother to a better facility if I could, but at this point every hospital in the city is overflowing." He looked at me with tired eyes. "Do you have somewhere to go?"

"I'm good. My aunt will take care of me till Mom gets out. She's at work right now."

It was a lie. I don't have an aunt. But the last thing the doc needed while trying to keep all these people alive was to have to worry about me. Besides, I had our apartment, and some good neighbors. I knew Martha-across-the-hall would give me a meal or two and John-up-the-street would do the same. So though I didn't have family-family, I had friends-family, and that was all I needed.

As it turned out, someone else was out looking for me . . . which was *not* the same as looking out for me.

That first night Martha fed me supper. The next day I went to visit John and got a good lunch. On the way home I bought some groceries with money from the cookie jar. That was only for emergencies, but I figured this qualified.

I also stopped to visit Mom. She was unconscious, so I couldn't talk to her. But she did squeeze my hand while I was holding hers, which gave me an insane amount of hope that she would be all right.

Things didn't get really bad until that night, when I was in the apartment on my own for the second time.

There was still no wind. The heat was crushing. Mom's condition hadn't changed. And I was freaking out.

I tried to relax. Seriously, I did. I even tried some deep breathing, which I had seen on some stupid TV show once.

It didn't work.

Finally I went into the kitchen and made myself a peanut butter sandwich. While I was eating it, I switched on the radio. A man's voice said, "The environmental crisis continues to grow steadily worse."

"Jerk," I muttered. "Anyone who has to breathe knows that."

The newscaster rattled on. "In accord with the governor's order, the last factories ceased production this morning. The air is so lethal that very few people are venturing into the streets. Area hospitals are so crowded with lung problems brought on by the crisis that new admissions are being placed on cots in the hallways."

I snapped off the radio. All I could think of was my mother, stuck in that clinic, struggling to breathe. Until the wind returned, there would be no improvement for her. She would only get worse and worse and . . .

I tried to shut out the thought. Getting to my feet, I paced the apartment, fear for my mother twisting my insides.

At the same time, my own longing for the wind was so strong I could almost believe Mom's story about the night I was born. It was as if some part of my soul had been yanked right out of me.

I opened the window and leaned against the sill, then thrust my head out into the night. "I want the wind!" I whispered. I drew back inside and fell to my knees as the truth crushed in on me. *I could not live without the wind.* For some reason I needed it in a way different from other people . . . not just to blow away the poison in the air, but to blow life into my heart.

An unexpected sound made me snap my head up.

I strained my ears and heard it again. Someone was singing! Singing, in this dark and hot and awful night. Even more, though I couldn't name it, the song was oddly familiar.

I went to the door, trying to hear it more clearly.

The singing grew closer. I heard a lift of beauty in the song that stirred me to wonder if things were not as bad as I had feared.

A moment later the voice was right outside the door.

Should I open it? Before I could decide, the door—which I knew was locked, because it locks automatically when you close it—burst inward.

An old man stepped through. He was short, barely taller than me, with long white hair and a crazy beard that reached to his waist. "There you are!" he cried. "You have no idea how hard it's been to find you!"

"I'm not going to a foster home!" I shouted, blurting out the fear that had consumed me since Mom had been admitted to the clinic.

The old man rolled his eyes. "Of course you're not going to a foster home. You're coming with me."

"Coming where? What are you talking about?"

He spread his hands as if the answer was obvious. "We have to rescue the wind!"

I backed away. "Who are you?"

He smiled. His teeth were remarkably white and straight. "My name is Zephron Windlord. I'm in charge of making the wind."

Great. Somehow I had attracted a nut. Or maybe a joker who had no sense of how awful everything really was.

The good news was, he didn't look dangerous—by which I mean he didn't have that look in his eyes you sometimes see in the street crazies.

On the other hand, his clothes were . . . unusual. He had on a silky blue shirt. Okay, that wasn't so strange. But over it he wore a fleecy vest—definitely not a good choice for the current heat situation! I noticed he wasn't the least bit sweaty. With that vest on, you would have thought his shirt would be soaked through! His pants, the color of a stormy sky, were loose and baggy, like Aladdin's in the movie. They were cinched at the waist with a dangling gold cord. The bottoms were tucked into high black boots.

Despite these oddities, it was his face that held my attention. He had piercing blue eyes that would have been frightening if he hadn't been looking at me with such obvious goodwill. His nose was arched, almost hawklike. The stern effect of that was softened by his thick, moon-white hair and his curling beard, which flowed all the way to his waist, looking like a captured waterfall. Despite the white hair, his face—which was the color of a new penny—was smooth and unwrinkled.

Then what he had said sank into my brain. "What do you mean, 'We have to rescue the wind'?"

Zephron's expression turned grim. "If you want to get technical, what we really have to rescue is Aerobellan."

It was my turn to roll my eyes. "Who is Aerobellan?"

"Not *who*. *What*. Aerobellan is the great horn I use to start the winds. It has been stolen, and unless we can get it back, there will be no more wind on earth. Ever." He took a deep breath, then added, "Which means that pretty much everyone and everything will die."

THE WINDHORN AT THE TOP OF THE WORLD

I stared at him. Then reality kicked in. "Oh, stop," I snapped. "I'm not a little kid. You don't make the wind. No one *makes* the wind. It just happens, because of the way things are. Air pressure and science and stuff like that."

The old man waved a hand in dismissal. "I know, I know. That's what you've been taught. And it's all right, because your teachers need to have something to believe in. But that doesn't alter the truth. The fact of the matter is, I seed the winds with Aerobellan, the great horn created for that task. Without those beginning gusts of air, the wind cannot happen."

"Even if that was true, which I don't think it is, what does it have to do with me?"

The old man looked at me in astonishment. "You don't know?"

"Know what?"

"The story of your birth."

"What do you know about the night I was born?" I demanded.

"Well, I was there, for one thing!" He waved a hand to ward off my next question. "We'll get to that in a minute. The first thing I need to make clear to you is that because my horn has been stolen, the world is in crisis. You must know that, Hurricane."

"How do you know my name?"

Ignoring my question, he continued, "It's not just the way pollution is poisoning the cities. Without the wind to move the clouds, the water that rises from the oceans, seas, and lakes will fall directly back to where it came from. Without wind to sweep the rains across the land, farms will dry up. Crops will die. Famine will follow and death will stalk the world."

I thought of my mother, weak and gasping in the clinic. Without the wind she would be dead before the rest of what Zephron was describing even happened.

"What can I do about it?" I said. "I can't even help my mom!"

"I'm sorry, Hurricane. I'm moving too fast. It's just that there is so much to tell you! Let's sit."

He gestured toward our old couch as if pointing toward a throne, then settled himself cross-legged at one end. I blinked. It almost appeared that he was sitting a fraction of an inch above it.

I sat at the opposite end.

"To start with," he said, "I live in a cave at the top of the world."

I snorted. "So you're telling me you live at the North Pole? Who are you, Santa Claus?"

"Don't be so self-centered. Living in the northern hemisphere, *you* might consider the North Pole the top of the world. From the outside, the South Pole has an equally valid claim to that title. Anyway, my home has a better claim for being the top, since it is located on the world's highest mountain."

"Now you're saying you live on Mount Everest?"

"Of course not! The mountain I live on is much higher than Everest."

"But . . ."

Zephron sighed. "I know, I know. You've been taught that Everest is the tallest mountain on Earth. That's fine. You *should* be taught that, since the mountain where I live has been hidden by magic for thousands of years."

"You can't hide a mountain!"

"Have you ever heard of it?"

"No."

"Well, then, we did a pretty good job, didn't we?"

Ignoring my skeptical face, Zephron said fiercely, "I'm not here to debate. Let me tell you what you need to know. My name is Zephron Windlord. I live in a cave at the top of the world. From there I bring the winds to life with Aerobellan, the Windhorn. At the back of my cave are seven doors. Each door leads to seven corridors, and each corridor leads to seven worlds. It has been many, many years since I have gone through one of those doors. However, it should not be forgotten that a door can work both ways. Yes?"

I nodded. At least I could agree on that.

"Last week I was preparing to take a nap. I had not slept in a month or so and I was tired."

I rolled my eyes but said nothing.

"I settled into my hammock. As I was drifting off, a prickle of magic washed over me. I sprang to my feet and saw a dark shape waving its hands in mystic gestures. I moved to defend myself but I was too late. Even as I raised my own hands, the shadowy creature finished its spell. Golden threads spun around me. Soon I was wrapped in what I can only call a cocoon . . . a cocoon that enclosed me from head to foot, holding me motionless."

"And then—" He stopped, and horror twisted his face. He closed his eyes and took a few breaths before resuming his story. "Then I toppled to the floor. I squirmed and struggled, but the cocoon held me tight. I do not know how much time passed—it felt like an eternity, but I suspect it was only a matter of minutes—before I screamed as I felt a piece of my soul being ripped away. In that moment I knew that whoever had cast this spell had stolen Aerobellan. Not only stolen the horn, but taken it clear out of this world.

"After that, I lost consciousness. I had no way of knowing how much time had passed before I finally woke. What I did know, instantly, was that the world was in mortal peril." He paused, then said, "I can see in your eyes that you think I'm crazy. I guarantee you that I'm not, though I did nearly fall into madness while I was held in that cocoon. The spell did finally release me. Whether that was due to my struggles, or because the magic had run its course, I cannot say. Weak and disoriented, I staggered to the horn's resting place.

"It was gone. Even though I had known to expect this, the emptiness I felt nearly crushed me. Hard on the heels of that feeling of loss came fear . . . fear for the entire world. I forced myself to settle and concentrate. Eyes closed, heart open, I tried to sense where the horn had gone. I *should* have been able to find it! Aerobellan is tied to me by bonds nearly as ancient and strong as those that hold the earth together. But I could not feel it, not a trace.

"My fear doubled. Not sense the horn? As well not sense my right hand! I suspect the thief's spell still surrounds me, that even now it is blocking my link to the horn. Which is why I have come for you, Hurricane."

I tensed, ready to bolt for the door if he tried to grab me. Surely I could outrun someone his age. But all I said was "I still don't understand."

He looked astonished. "Haven't you figured it out? You are tied to the horn! Oh, not as strongly as I was. But tied to it nonetheless. You have been, from the night of your birth."

This was the second time he had mentioned this. "What do you know about the night I was born?"

He seemed surprised. "You *have* been told the story, haven't you?"

"Yes, but . . ."

Zephron closed his eyes and shook his head. "Ah. You thought it was a story your mother had invented. Well, that explains why you're having a hard time accepting me. Yes, it is a story. But it's a true one. I should know, since I was there."

I shook my head. "No one was there but my mother and my grandmother."

"They were with you in the house. *I* was riding the wind above you. When the storm tore the house from over your mother's head, I watched you come squalling into the world, a tiny, wrinkled bundle of possibility. So I protected you, guiding the worst of the winds away from you. Even so, parts of that storm were beyond my control." A smile flickered over his lips. "That *was* a storm. Magic surged through it, tumbling and sweeping across the earth as it rarely does these days. And that magic was in the gentle breezes I sent to soothe you."

He looked directly into my eyes. "When those breezes entered you, entered with your first breaths, they made themselves a part of you, and claimed you with their magic." He stopped, frowned, then said, "At least, I think this is so. My heart believes that when the magic of the wind and the horn came to you that night they nestled into your very soul.

"Why do you think your yearning for the wind is so fierce, Hurricane? It's because the wind is part of you! It's in your blood and bone and marrow. Without the wind you will die. Not the death from stagnation and starvation that's coming to everyone. You'll die inside, the way I am dying even now."

His voice went gentle. "Our suffering is the same, my boy. But it's only suffering. What counts is that because of the magic that seeped into you the night of your birth, you can do what is no longer possible for me. *You* can sense Aerobellan, sense the path it has followed. The horn will call to you. I know it will. It has to!"

This was the most ridiculous thing I had ever heard. Yet how could this old man have known about the night of my birth? And what else had ever explained my strange connection to the wind?

"Am I the only one?" I asked. "Hasn't anyone else been touched by the wind?"

"Yes, a few. But that was long ago. As magic has become less welcome in the world, it has become rare for me to venture out from my mountaintop as I did that night. The others, the ones still alive, are far too old for such a trip."

I sat in silence, overwhelmed by all this. Wasn't I too *young* for it?

"Don't you want to come?" asked Zephron.

Of course I wanted to go with him! But this had to be a dream. Where was the truth? What could I believe?

"We've wasted enough time," Zephron said, his voice now forceful. "Come with me."

Still swinging between hopeful belief and realistic scorn, I decided it would be safer to continue to humor him. Easier, to tell the truth.

"Where are we going?" I asked as he led me out the door.

"To the top of the world."

"And how are we going to get there?"

"Shamoondra will take us."

"Who's Shamoondra?" I asked. *And who gave someone a name like that?* I wondered.

"You'll see."

Zephron led me to the stair that goes to the roof. New fear rose inside me. What if he was crazy after all and was planning to fling me off the building? But he was behind me on the stairs, and I didn't want to try to get back down past him. So I stepped through the door at the top of the stairs.

The half-moon, barely visible through the brownish haze, provided a feeble light.

A slight sound from behind caused me to turn.

That was when reality came crashing down around my ears.

4

SHAMOONDRA

I yelped and grabbed Zephron's sleeve.

He chuckled and said, "Don't worry, she won't hurt you."

She was a tiger.

To make things worse, *this* tiger was unlike anything ever seen in a zoo . . . or anywhere else, as far as I knew. To begin with, she was huge, standing at least six feet at the shoulder, which was a full foot above my face. But her size wasn't the strangest thing. The strangest thing was the feathered ebony wings that stretched from her shoulders—wings too impossible to be real . . . and too real to be impossible.

I stood stock-still, worried that the slightest movement might rouse the tiger's hunting instincts.

"Beautiful, isn't she?" Zephron murmured.

"She's yours?" I whispered.

"I wouldn't call her mine, exactly. But she stays with me. 'Friend' would be a better word. She's a friend."

"Is she safe?"

Zephron smiled. "She's not going to eat you, if that's what you're worried about."

"That's good to know. But how can this be real? Am I dreaming?"

"Stop clinging to illusions and let in the truth," Zephron replied sharply. "Shamoondra is here. She is real. I am also real and need your help. Are you going to accept the reality of your own story or not?"

I turned toward him and studied his ice-blue eyes and smooth bronze face carefully. What I saw scared me. But it also made up my mind.

"All right. I'm with you."

Zephron smiled. "That's better. You have a strong gaze, by the way. Now it's time to introduce you."

Taking me by the arm, he led me to Shamoondra's side.

The great cat turned her head and stared at me. Her enormous yellow eyes were bigger than my fists. I thought of the words from Mom's story: *The last thing I remember was two golden eyes staring down at me from the storm.*

Encouraged by Zephron's hand on my shoulder, I did not drop my gaze. Finally the tiger lowered her head, then curled out her enormous tongue and licked my face. It was like having a warm, soggy, and very rough towel pulled over my cheeks.

"Hey!" I cried. "Cut that out!"

Shamoondra purred, a rumble so powerful I could feel the vibrations in my chest.

Zephron laughed. "You've just been tested, Hurricane, in much the way you were testing me a moment ago. You passed inspection. Shamoondra will carry you."

I felt a surge of excitement at the idea of riding this enormous creature. If I *was* going crazy, this was definitely the way to do it!

Zephron spoke a phrase that I could not understand. Shamoondra crouched, then spread her wings to make room for us. Zephron scrambled up. He moved more quickly than I would have thought possible, given how old he looked. He extended his hand to me. I took it. He gave a pull, again surprising me with his strength. An instant later I was sitting behind him, on the back of a giant winged tiger!

We were just behind the spot where Shamoondra's wings joined her shoulders. When she folded her wings partway, it was as if a tent had enclosed us.

"Buckle up," said Zephron. "It's going to be a long journey."

That was the first I noticed the set of straps and buckles wrapped around the tiger's belly. With Zephron's help I secured myself. Once firmly in place, I asked, "Don't you need a bridle or something? You know, to guide her and tell her when to stop and stuff?"

"She knows the way," Zephron replied. "Knows it better than I do, in fact. And she understands when I speak to her." Turning to look ahead, he shouted, "Hyazakkim Hai!"

The great cat shot forward, hurtled across the roof, then leaped over the edge.

I screamed as we plummeted toward the street. But when Shamoondra leaped, she also spread those enormous ebony wings. They caught the air and our descent slowed, then stopped. Then she pumped her wings to lift us upward. A wild joy surged in my veins. I was flying on the back of a great winged tiger, perched behind a man who was the master of the winds!

As we glided, smooth and silent, above the buildings, I looked down at my dying city. The delight I felt in flying faded. The streets were dark and quiet. Millions of people were down there, praying for the wind to return and sweep away the poison we ourselves had pumped into the air.

Then I thought not of the millions but of the one: my mother lying in her bed in that clinic, struggling to breathe. A fist closed around my heart. Like all of those millions, she was depending on me, waiting for me to find the horn that would bring back the wind and save her life. I felt dizzy. Even if this *was* real, wasn't it too much to ask of an old man and a boy?

We were higher now and I was suddenly aware that nothing save the body of the tiger was between me and the world below. I felt dizzy. And still we rose. As we continued upward the air went from a welcome coolness to bitter cold. I wondered how long the journey was going to be . . . and if I would freeze before it was over.

"Brace yourself," called Zephron. "In a minute or so we'll leave the fields you know and enter the Enchanted Realm."

"The what?"

"It's complicated," Zephron answered, as if everything else going on wasn't. "Think of it as a world that overlaps the world you know. The Enchanted Realm is where magic and the majority of magical beings reside. The human world largely rejects magic these days. Even so, magic still clusters around the places where humans are most present. We're heading west. As we pass over the Great Plains, and later when we pass over the ocean, the Enchanted Realm will be smaller than the human world. Which will shorten our journey."

"Oh," I said, though what he said sounded mathematically impossible. Before I could say more, light exploded around me. Suddenly everything was different. For one thing, I was no longer cold, which was a nice change.

"Welcome to the Enchanted Realm," said Zephron, as if that explained everything.

The combination of the straps holding me secure and the pleasant warmth let me start to relax. Gazing down, I was able to marvel at the beauty of the world passing below.

The skies were clear and cloudless. The moon, which at home had been only a half-moon, was now nearly full and shining brighter than I had ever seen it. Before long we were sailing above high mountains, their peaks etched against the sky by the moon's silver light. The silence was broken by a high-pitched shriek somewhere to our right. I looked toward the sound and cried out when I saw a winged creature heading toward us.

"Be silent," cautioned Zephron.

I bit my lips and watched as the creature drew nearer. I had to clamp down twice as hard to keep from crying out again when I realized that what I saw was a griffin. An actual griffin—feathered eagle head, furred lion body and all! I had drawn plenty of griffins. I had never dreamed I would see one!

Shamoondra let out a yowl. The griffin drew closer. I wondered if it was going to attack. But when it was no more than ten yards away it tipped its wings and banked so it could circle us. Shamoondra yowled again. The griffin screeched back, circled us twice more, then switched course and flew away.

"It was just checking to make sure we were only passing through," Zephron explained. "Griffins are very protective of their space."

"Thanks for explaining," I said, once I could breathe again.

After that I lost track of time. Or maybe time lost track of me. For whatever reason, it didn't seem as if nearly enough of it had gone by before we left the mountains behind and came to the ocean, where the sky was covered by clouds so dense they obscured most of the moonlight.

"Why are the clouds so thick?" I asked.

"Because there's no wind to move them after they rise from the water," Zephron answered.

Now I understood what Zephron had tried to explain before, and felt the danger not just in my head but in my gut. Without the wind, the clouds could not move. Unmoving, they would never leave the sea to pass over the land. Instead, they would remain exactly where they were . . . which meant the water they held would fall straight back to the water from which it had risen. Which meant that as far as land areas were concerned, not only was wind gone, so was rain.

Unless we regained the horn, the world would dry out and die.

We continued to fly between layers of gray—smooth gray water below, heavy gray clouds above. The only sound was the swoosh of Shamoondra's seemingly tireless wings. That changed when a melancholy cry rose from below us.

"What was that?" I asked nervously.

"Humpback whale. Or maybe a sea serpent. Hard to tell with everything being so dark."

Then, as if he understood my feeling of being trapped in all this grayness, Zephron spoke a few words to Shamoondra. She angled the direction of our flight, sending us up into the clouds.

It felt weird to move through air so thick and moist, heavier than the heaviest fog I had ever experienced. I strained my eyes but it was impossible to tell how far into the clouds I could see. It was as if everything, the world itself, had disappeared and we were the only solid things in it.

As we continued up, the thick mist grew luminous. When we burst out of it, into the world *above* the clouds, I gasped. The moon was so bright it was almost like day. Its cool white light illuminated the cloud landscape below . . . a roll of hills and valleys and mountains that looked oddly solid now that we were above them. It was like an alternate world, so real it seemed it should be filled with people and plants and animals.

"Look up," said Zephron.

I raised my eyes. The sky above was black velvet, spattered with more stars than could ever be seen from the streets of Chicago.

"I had no idea," I whispered.

Zephron chuckled. "How could you?"

I don't know how long we flew above the clouds. I just know it was a good thing I was strapped in, because at some point I fell asleep, leaning against the Windlord's back.

Another tingle skittering through my body woke me.

"What was that?" I cried.

"We just left the Enchanted Realm," said Zephron.

The clouds had vanished and we were now flying above a range of snowcapped mountains. The rising sun shone so brightly off the white peaks that it hurt my eyes.

"We've traveled west for so long that we're now in what you think of as the East," Zephron said.

My sleepy brain had to work on that for a minute before it made sense.

Shamoondra headed upward yet again, beating her wings to lift us higher and higher. I leaned around Zephron. We were nearing the peak of a mountain that towered above the others. As we soared over it I saw that the top was flat, a near-perfect circle several yards across.

On one side of the circle a square of wood was set level with the surface. Chains stretched from the wood to an odd device that had some big gears and a large crank.

More important, however, was the silvery metal frame in the very center of the circle. My stomach twisted. I was certain that frame had been built to hold the Windlord's Horn, Aerobellan.

It was empty.

5

THE CAVE
OF THE WINDS

Shamoondra circled down and landed close to the wooden square. At a word from Zephron she crouched. Quickly the Windlord unbuckled himself and slid from her side. I had to figure out how to get out of the straps that held me in place before I could follow.

I expected to feel the bite of frigid air once I left the tiger's side. To my surprise, the mountaintop was warm. Reading the puzzled look on my face, Zephron said, "Magic can be a wonderful thing."

"Why can't you magic up some wind?" I asked.

He scowled. "Warming a bubble of air not much bigger than a house is quite different from providing wind for an entire world!"

I nodded and turned my attention to the frame. As I did, I felt a faint tingle and a hint of longing. Was it the sense of the horn that Zephron had been talking about?

I examined the frame. Its base, resting on the smooth

stone of the mountaintop, was an open circle about three feet across. From this circle four flat pieces of metal, obviously meant to keep the contraption stable, extended for several feet across the stone. Four straight poles, each as high as my shoulder, rose from the joints where these feet were attached to the circle. These uprights were held together by another metal ring, the same size as the base. Four more pipes angled outward and upward from the spots where the poles joined the upper ring. Each of these pipes, which were about two feet long, ended in an upturned half circle.

"This was where I stood to play the horn," said Zephron. He closed his eyes and sighed. "I wish you could have seen it, Hurricane. It is a wondrous thing, gold and smooth and made to give birth to the winds." His hands cut the air, describing the shape. "The mouthpiece stretches into a slender tube that, inches later, divides into four tubes that curl about themselves, growing wider and wider until they blossom into great bell shapes, one for each of the four great winds."

He stroked one of the upturned half circles. "The base of each bell rested in one of these curves. I would stand in the middle of it all and bring the winds to life, using the keys and stops built into the tubes to create a thousand variations."

Zephron's description was so vivid that I could almost see the horn—which made the loss of it all the more painful. The Windlord gazed at the empty frame for a moment longer, then shook himself and said, "We should go inside."

He crossed to the device beside the wooden square and began to turn the crank. As the square tipped up I realized that it was a door. When the upper edge was high enough, I saw, in the dim light that shone from below, a curved ramp made of black stone.

"Stairs would have been difficult for Shamoondra," Zephron said as he stepped toward the opening.

We descended single file—the Windlord, then me, with the tiger padding along behind. Though she had just carried me halfway around the world, I couldn't ignore the fact that to her I must look snack-sized.

I stopped worrying about Shamoondra when we reached the bottom of the ramp and stepped into Zephron's cave. I caught my breath. The place was perfect, somehow like the home I had always wanted without even knowing I wanted it. Being in it felt . . . *right*.

"Do you like it?" asked Zephron.

I nodded, not yet ready to speak.

While I stood gawking, Shamoondra walked past me to Zephron. With quick movements he removed the harness that had kept us safely in place. As he went to hang it on a peg that extended from the cave wall, the tiger shook herself, then strolled to the left wall of the cave, where a broad niche held a crackling fire. She folded her wings neatly across her back, settled onto the hearth, sighed heavily, and began to purr. The low rumble felt comforting somehow.

"She's tired," said Zephron. "It's been years since either of us ventured into the outer world and it was a long journey. She's getting too old for this sort of thing." He sighed and added, "In truth, so am I. But it had to be done."

I gazed around, trying to take it all in. Some light came from the fireplace, but most came from four smokeless torches mounted in the walls. At the front of the cave an opening to the outside world provided even more light. I saw a wide ledge there, almost like a front porch.

"Doesn't that opening let in a lot of cold air?" I asked.

Zephron smiled. "It's shielded by a heat barrier. It's very effective."

By this time, an invisible heat barrier didn't surprise me.

In the middle of the cave a wooden table, round and solid-looking, held a brown pitcher, a loaf of dark bread, and a chunk of cheese twice the size of my fist. Beside them was a bowl of fruit. Two wooden plates and a pair of thick candles that shed a low but steady light across the food completed the picture.

The wall to the right of the table held another large niche, this one with a hammock slung inside. A small space carved at one end of the niche contained another candle. At the other end, not in the niche but in the cave itself, a wooden rack about four feet high supported a small collection of scrolls. They looked ancient, some yellowing, a few even torn. Despite that, I felt certain that Zephron must treat them with care.

To the right of the ramp where we had entered, the

cave extended into the mountain. How far it went was impossible to say, since the light only reached partway in. But I had no doubt that before long that was where we would be heading.

"Are you hungry?" Zephron asked.

"Yes!" I said, startling myself with how loudly I spoke. The question had made me realize that I was, in fact, famished.

Zephron led me to the table. I sat but continued to study the cave. Chicago seemed far away—almost as if that was the fantasy world and where I sat now was the true reality. My fingers fairly itched with the desire for a pencil and some drawing paper. Shamoondra by the fireplace would make a great picture.

On the wall to the right of the fireplace hung a tapestry. Though it was old and somewhat faded, I could make out the image, which seemed to show this very cave, with two people in it. One looked like Zephron but considerably younger. The other was taller and grander. Passing from one to the other was a golden object that was obviously the Windlord's Horn.

Zephron slid a milk-filled mug at me. I took a sip. It was warm, which normally would have grossed me out. But this milk was so rich that I didn't mind. Even so, it would have been better with chocolate.

Next he sliced some cheese, put a few pieces on each of the wooden plates, then pushed one toward me. I looked at the cheese in the center of the table and blinked. Despite how much the Windlord had sliced off, it remained the same size.

He tore a hunk from the bread, then pushed the loaf across the table. I followed his example and tore off a piece for myself. I put the bread back. When I looked at it again, it was also the same size it had been before. It was like a fairy tale!

I had been chewing for a few minutes when I looked up and saw Zephron staring at me.

"What now?" I asked, to break the silence.

"We pack. Then, when you feel ready, we go see if you really can sense the trail of the horn."

"You seemed way more sure of that when you were trying to talk me into coming here!"

"Let us pray to the Powers Bright that I was right!"

With that he stood and crossed the cave, saying, "We'll have to travel lightly. We can bring the clothes we have on and another set for you for extreme cold. That's about all the garb we can allow ourselves. Everything else will have to be food and gear." Standing on tiptoe, he reached up to a hook that held a heavy parka. "Got this years ago," he said as he lifted it down. "Someday I'll tell you the story."

"Aren't we going to need two of those?" I asked.

He looked startled, then laughed. "No. This one is for you, in case the trail takes us someplace very cold. Temperature is not much of an issue for me."

"I should have figured," I muttered.

Zephron moved quickly around the cave, opening

storage spaces I would never have suspected were there. Soon the parka had been joined by a pair of quilted pants and two pairs of boots. When I raised an eyebrow at that, Zephron said, "I'll need boots in case of snow."

Next came two lanterns.

"How do you turn these on?" I asked, looking for some kind of switch.

"Just hold one up and say 'Light.'"

I tried it. Instantly the lantern began to glow. That was good, though some magical word would have been cooler.

"Saying 'Dark' will turn it off," added Zephron, rolling up the parka. "Keep one of them out—we'll need it soon. If you look in the storage space below the tapestry you'll find some twine. Fetch it, please."

I brought back the twine, which we used to keep each item of clothing rolled as tightly as possible. We finished packing in silence, tucking in useful things like rope, a small hatchet, a blanket, and some matches.

Once we had those in place, Zephron produced great quantities of food from a number of unexpected caches. We filled the rest of the space in the packs with cheeses sealed in red wax, dried fruit, leathery strips of dried meat, and bottles of water.

"Couldn't we just bring the bread and cheese from the table?" I asked. "I mean, it's magic food that never runs out, right?"

"Well, yes and no. It never runs out *here*. But the magic

6

THE GREEN SPHERE

When we entered the dark area at the back of the cave Zephron lifted the lantern we had kept out and said, "Light!" In the sudden glow I saw that the opening narrowed to a tunnel.

We followed this tunnel for several minutes. Finally I saw a new flicker ahead, and soon we entered a cave lit by four torches. Like the ones in Zephron's cave, they were smokeless.

In their light I saw seven doors, each unique in the way it was designed and carved.

"Who lit the torches?" I asked, wondering if Zephron had somehow managed it from a distance.

"I don't know," he replied. "They've been burning here for as long as I have occupied the main cave. They never go out."

He looked at me expectantly.

I took a breath and stared at the dark doors. They were

made of wide planks joined by strong crossbars. The nails, hinges, and handles were enormous. They looked very old, and very solid.

Up until now, I had felt a pull from the horn. But it was general, a kind of *I was here, but now I am gone. Can you follow me?*

Now I needed to find a more direct connection, to sense the exact path it had taken.

I glanced back at Zephron. He nodded encouragement.

Closing my eyes, I opened my heart, aching to catch the trail of Aerobellan. But what should I feel? What should I be looking for, if that was the word? How was I supposed to find this trail? It wouldn't be by sight or sound or anything else I was used to.

I walked to the door in front of me, the center door, hoping that being closer would help.

Nothing.

I leaned against the door, spread my arms so my chest was flat on the wood, held my breath.

Nothing.

I turned to Zephron and shook my head. He gestured to the door farthest to my left. I nodded. It made sense to try the doors in order. I stepped to the far-left door and pressed myself against it, then reached out with all the longing I felt for the wind.

Nothing.

I moved to the next door and did the same. I tried to

stay calm, to remind myself that Zephron believed I could do this.

I felt nothing. *No need to panic,* I told myself. *There are still four doors left.*

The Windlord put a hand on my shoulder. He was silent but I took the message of support, nodded, and moved to the next door. Pressing myself against it, I waited as I had in front of the others, straining to catch . . . what?

I felt nothing.

I passed the center door, which I had already tried, and walked on to the fifth door. The moment I touched it, my fingers began to tingle . . . a tingle that raced up my arms and flowed into my body. *This* was the door through which the thief had taken the horn.

"I've got it!" I cried. *"I've got it!"*

I didn't realize how worried I had been under my hope until that moment of certainty.

"What now?" I whispered . . . then felt silly, because who was there to hear except Zephron? Yet something about all this seemed to make whispering a good idea.

Zephron drew me gently aside, then opened the door.

Beyond lay a dark tunnel.

"Go cautiously now," Zephron said. "You're going to come to a stairway in a little while."

He lifted his lantern as I stepped through the door. The tunnel walls were so smooth that I wondered if they were natural or if someone had carved them. A slight spicy scent filled the air.

After a few minutes the lantern revealed a steep set of steps going down. If each of the seven doors led to seven corridors, and each corridor to seven caves, things might get crowded on the mountaintop. So it would make sense if the corridors were placed at different levels.

I don't know how many steps we went down before we came to another cave. It seemed like umpty-kabillion. The spicy scent—it was like cinnamon, but mixed with something else I couldn't name—grew more intense.

When we finally came to the bottom of the steps Zephron muttered a few words. A band of blue light about the width of my hand lit up around the walls, revealing a large open space.

On the far side were the openings to the seven corridors.

I walked to the cave's center, closed my eyes, held my breath . . . and was caught almost instantly by the pull of the horn. I had no doubts anymore: I could track Aerobellan.

Zephron followed me as I walked to the corridor farthest to the left.

Before we entered, he stopped and said, "Dark!" Instantly, the lantern went out, as did the band of blue light, leaving us in the deepest darkness I had ever known.

"Better this way," Zephron said softly, as if understanding the question on my lips. "Place your left hand on the wall and keep following your sense of the horn."

The stone was pleasant to the touch: smooth, dry, and cool. The spicy smell grew even more distinct. Before long the darkness began to fade. After we had walked for a few minutes, I saw a soft glow ahead. It pulsed in a steady rhythm, growing dimmer, then slowly brightening again.

"We have almost reached this tunnel's grotto," Zephron said, his voice as hushed as if we were stepping into a church or library. "That's where we'll find the entry points to the seven worlds."

The light was not directly ahead but shining onto a rock wall from somewhere else. Then the tunnel made a sharp turn. We rounded the corner, and I stopped in my tracks.

We had entered a cavern much larger than Zephron's cave. In its center was a wide pool whose surface danced with colored light. On the far side of the pool was the source of those colors: seven globes of liquid light, each about ten feet in diameter.

"Whoa!" I said.

"I understand," replied Zephron. "As many times as I have seen these grottoes, their beauty never fails to take my breath away."

"But where are the doors?" I asked, baffled.

"Those spheres *are* the doors. Step through any of them and you will find yourself in another world."

The spheres rose in an arc that stretched from the

floor on the left to the peak of the cavern on the right. Each sphere glowed with a single color of the rainbow, starting with red on the left and rising to violet on the right. The colors, intense and pure, reflected from the stalactites and stalagmites, making the cavern appear to be pierced with swords of light. A curved stone stairway in front of the spheres matched their rise. From that stairway extended seven short bridges, each leading to the edge of a sphere.

"Have you ever gone through one?" I asked.

"Many times. But that was long ago."

"What was it like?"

"Fascinating, frightening, and fabulous. But this is not the time to talk about that. We need to move on."

"Will there be people?"

"Possibly, though there is no telling what they might look like."

"How will we talk to them?"

Zephron smiled. "*That* question I can answer! One of the wonders of the spheres is that with passage comes a gift of language. Once through, you will speak like a native of the world we enter. It will be so natural you won't even notice it unless you really try. Then it can be quite startling to hear the sounds that will come out of your mouth."

"But how . . . ?"

He shook his head. "I have no idea how it works. It

took a magic more potent than anything I know to create the spheres to begin with."

I nodded and let the pull of the horn take over. It led me to circle the pool and then move up the stairs to the fourth sphere, the green one. Gazing into it, I felt as if I was seeing all the greens of all the springs the world had ever known, the green of budding trees and new-sprouted grass, of unripe apples and cool forest depths, the greens I suddenly remembered from before our move to Chicago, all mingled into one perfect color.

I stepped onto the bridge but Zephron took my arm and pulled me back, saying, "I need to do something before we enter."

I was so eager to keep going that I had to fight down a wave of frustration at being stopped.

Zephron slipped off his pack, set it on the stone stair, then pulled the piece of wood he had called a time peg from his belt. He moved onto the little bridge. About three feet along the way he knelt and ran his fingers across its surface. "Ah," I heard him mutter. "Good."

He pressed the peg into the bridge. Since the bridge was made of stone and the peg of wood, I figured that when he moved his hands he had been looking for a hole that was already there . . . though, given how much magic was going on, he might just have been looking for the right spot.

About two inches of the peg showed above the stone.

"Now will you tell me what that does?" I asked.

"Certainly. We are about to reenter the Enchanted Realm, which is where the spheres exist. The time peg will lock us to the moment we step into the green sphere. When we return, assuming we are successful and *do* return, we will come back at the exact moment that we left."

For the first time I felt we could do all this and still get back in time to save my mother! Then I realized something else. With an edge of anger in my voice, I asked, "Why didn't you use that peg before we left Chicago? Or better yet, before you came looking for me?"

"Think back, Hurricane. When did we enter the Enchanted Realm on our trip here?"

"Well, I can't tell you the exact time, but Shamoondra took off and we were flying and . . . oh."

"Exactly," he said. "This peg has to be placed—usually pounded, but with the spheres the holes are already in place—at the spot where you pass from the human world to the Enchanted Realm, or vice versa. On my journey, both ways, that passage happened in midair. If I had tried to place the peg then, it would simply have fallen to earth and been lost. Placing it here is the best I can manage."

I nodded, torn between being thrilled that we could return at this exact moment and wishing for more, that we could have linked our return to the instant we left the roof of the Jerrold Arms. In my mind I heard my mother say, "Gratitude is better than greed, Hurricane. If someone gives you an apple, don't wish they had given you two. Be glad for the apple you have."

I stepped onto the bridge. Then, side by side, Zephron and I walked into the green sphere.

part two

OTHER WORLDS

THE DYING RIVER

Green poured into me, filling me with springtime, and leaves, and asparagus (okay, that wasn't so great) and then . . . and then it was over.

I was standing in a cave. It didn't take long to see that it was a different cave, smaller and darker than the one we had left. It took a second more to realize another thing, a terrifying thing.

I was alone.

I turned and stared at the green sphere. Any second Zephron would step out of it. He had to!

He didn't.

I was on the edge of a complete freak-out. Fortunately, the pull of the horn brought me back. I simply had to find Zephron, and then we could move on. I took a few deep breaths, then decided to walk around the sphere to see if he was on the other side. Maybe he had stumbled and knocked himself out.

It turned out that walking around the sphere was impossible; it filled the cave from wall to wall.

"Zephron?" I called. "Are you stuck over there?"

No answer.

The only thing that made sense was to go back through the sphere to see what had gone wrong. I took another deep breath, then stepped in. Again I was surrounded by green. But after walking just a few steps I emerged not in the cavern of the spheres but in what seemed to be the same narrow cave. The only difference was that now I was on the other side of the sphere.

Still no sign of Zephron.

All right, first thing to do was to get back to the other side of the sphere. I stepped into it again and was instantly back where I had first come out. Which made it clear that I was stranded.

Maybe the thing needs some time to recharge, I told myself.

I sat down to think and all too soon came to an unwelcome conclusion: Zephron or not, I would have to keep going. If Zephron could have come through, he would have. So something had gone wrong. I still had my pack and I could still sense the horn. Therefore, I had to keep going. I had to get to the horn and figure out how to get back. I would worry about one thing at a time. So . . . horn first.

Ahead—that is, walking away from the sphere—and somewhat above, I could see a circle of daylight. I started toward it. The cave floor sloped up at a sharp angle and after a while I was panting. Then I came to a solid wall of stone. Refusing to panic, I told myself there had to be a way out. I felt along the wall and found a set of indentations that had to be hand- and footholds. Who had carved them? Had he or she done this journey once, or many times?

A twenty-foot climb took me to the top of the cliff. I hoisted myself onto a flat space. Now I was only about ten feet from the opening. I started forward, and when I finally stepped out of the tunnel I heaved a huge sigh of relief. I now stood on a hillside that sloped down to a valley. The landscape here was more yellow than green, yet still looked cool and pleasant.

To my right the towers of a distant city rose against the sky. So there were people here! Or, if not people, at least some kind of beings advanced enough to build those towers. I was fascinated by the idea of going to the city. Unfortunately, I could tell that Aerobellan's trail led in the other direction.

And then . . . and then . . . I felt a touch of wind! As the breeze brushed past me, my heart surged with joy. The feeling vanished almost instantly. It was not the right kind of wind . . . not Windhorn wind.

Did different worlds have different windhorns? Or did this world get its wind some other way? Zephron would probably know.

A pang of missing him stopped me in my tracks. What had happened to him? Was he trapped someplace between the worlds? Had the green sphere taken him to another world entirely? Could whoever had stolen the horn control the spheres that way?

What kept me from completely losing it was that I was positive I was in the right world. Even if that wind hadn't come from Aerobellan, I was dead certain the horn had come this way. Pulled by my sense of it, I looked to my left.

The view that way was more forbidding. The hill where I stood was at the lower edge of a series of foothills. The grassland gradually gave way to tree-covered slopes that ended at a line of cliffs, which cupped the far end of the valley like a hand of stone. The cliffs were much taller than the towers of the city, and something about them made me feel that they were home to many mysteries.

I shuddered and looked directly ahead, down to the valley—the route the thief had taken. Cutting through the valley was what looked to be the bed of a great river. Except the river itself was mostly gone and only a slender stream ran between the wide banks. Something glimmered on both banks, but I couldn't make out what it was.

The water flowed toward the city. Looking the other way, upstream, I saw that the stream emerged from the forest, where close-packed trees stood like giant foot soldiers guarding the cliffs.

How long was this going to take? Praying that the time peg would do its job—the fact that Zephron had disappeared had shaken my faith in him—I started forward. It didn't take long to realize that the trail of the horn did not lead straight down the hill but instead angled toward the forest and the cliffs. No path had been worn through the knee-length grass, so it wasn't a trail that anyone followed on a regular basis. Clearly the thief, and only the thief, had gone this way.

It was hot and the tall grass rustled around my legs, sending up a pleasant odor that reminded me of the hay-fields back in Mississippi. The soft chirr of insects filled the air. I heard an occasional scuttle as some small animal hurried away from me.

I smelled the trouble before I saw it, but exactly *what* I was smelling wasn't clear. Something was dead and rotting, that much was certain. The stink grew stronger as I approached the river—though as the terrain leveled out I could no longer actually see the river, because it was lined by large trees whose slender branches swept the ground, blocking my view.

The trees were not quite willows. Even so, they had the same blade-shaped leaves and gracefully drooping limbs I remembered so well from trees that grew by the creek near where we had lived before moving to Chicago.

A dirt road ran along the edge of the trees. The road indicated people. Of course, I already knew there were people here, because of the city. What I still didn't know was what *kind* of people. People like me? People who were only sort of people? Or some kind of strange beings that

I would barely recognize as people? Heck, for all I knew this might not be a road at all, just the track of some giant worm!

Curiosity led me to push through the trees toward the riverbed. As I parted the slender branches to step through, I discovered a large open area, at least twenty feet wide, beneath the trees. It was like stepping under a giant umbrella. I could hear a buzzing sound now but couldn't figure out where it was coming from. Also, the smell was getting worse.

I crossed the open space and pushed through the next layer of branches. What I saw made me gag. Closest to the edge of the bank the riverbed was dry and cracked, but also bare. It was at about fifteen feet out that the death began. There thousands—maybe *tens* of thousands—of dead fish stretched in both directions. The smell was overwhelming. My stomach turned as I realized that the shiny ribbon I had noticed from the top of the slope was made of millions of insects swarming over the dead fish. Disgusted, I pushed back through the trees to the road. But I was haunted by the sight. What did it mean? Was this some kind of annual die-off? Or was this world facing some environmental crisis of its own?

I shook myself and tried to get my imagination under control. Then I let my sense of the horn pull me along.

After what seemed like a couple of hours I heard a sound ahead. I stopped for a moment, trying to figure out what was making it. But the sound was muffled and I wasn't close enough yet. I walked on, trying not to make any noise myself.

When I had gone a little farther I realized the sound was coming from the riverbed. Since the drooping trees obscured my view, I left the road and once more pushed my way through the slender branches. I crossed the open area and stepped between some of the branches on the far side so I could see the riverbed. Again, I was struck by the stench of the dead fish.

Then I saw the source of the sound. About fifty feet from what had been the edge of the river, submerged in mud nearly to his shoulders, was a manlike creature struggling to pull himself back to level ground. Given the cracked, drying mud that surrounded him, I wondered how he could possibly have sunk so far into the riverbed.

I say "manlike" because though he had a head and two arms (that was all I could see of him at the moment), his face was like nothing I had ever seen. His head was not much bigger than mine, but his eyes were easily the size of tennis balls. His nose—well, he didn't really have a nose, just a couple of slits where his nostrils should be. His mouth was twice as wide as you would expect, nearly splitting his face. His head was hairless, his skin a mottled brownish green.

I felt I should do something to help. Without even thinking, I stepped out from the cover of the branches. The frog-man spotted me at once and shouted, "Boy, don't just stand there like a fool! Help!"

"How?" I cried.

Even from where I stood I could see him roll those enormous eyes. "Find something to pull me out with! The mud is solid almost all the way out, so it's safe to walk on. Just don't get too close to me!"

My first thought was to look for a fallen branch. Then I had a better idea. I shucked my pack and dug out the rope Zephron had given me back in his cave.

I held it up for the frog-man to see.

"Excellent!" he croaked.

Moving cautiously, I walked out into the riverbed. The strange man had spoken the truth—the drying mud was solid. But the stink of the fish made me want to puke. It was even worse when I had to start picking my way between them . . . or in some places walk right on them.

When I was about ten feet from the froggy-looking guy he called, "Don't get any closer! Toss me the rope!"

Holding one end, I threw the coil in his direction. It went too far to his left. At the same time I heard a gurgling sound and saw muddy bubbles popping all around him.

As they did, he sank another few inches into the muck.

8

URBANG GARGLACK

"Again!" cried the frog-man urgently. "Fast! Fast, boy!"

I drew the rope back, coiling it as I did, then flung it toward him once more. This time it fell close enough for him to grab.

"Now pull!"

I pulled as hard as I could but he was held tight by the muck. Worse, he was pulling at the same time. Rather than drawing him *out* of the muck, that was pulling me toward it! He realized the problem and gasped, "Not going to work. I'll hold on to this end. You go back and wrap the rest around the tree. That way I will have something solid to pull against."

"I don't think the rope will be long enough!"

"We won't know until you try, and if you don't try soon it will be too late!"

I fed out the rope as I slogged back across the mud. I hadn't gone more than twenty feet when I could tell for sure that there wouldn't be enough. At least, that was what I thought until I felt the rope grow warm in my hands. I couldn't actually see it get longer as I continued across the mud, then scrambled up the bank and under the curtain of leaves. But I had enough rope to keep going. Soon I had it wrapped twice around the trunk of the tree—something that used at least twelve feet of rope all by itself.

"All set!" I shouted. "See if you can pull yourself out!"

At once the rope stretched taut. I braced myself against the trunk, hoping I could hold my end in place. As it turned out, the tree's bark was rough enough to keep the rope in place. Or who knows . . . maybe the rope itself was doing that. It was clearly magical.

I heard the frog-man gasping and panting but I didn't dare let go to check on his progress, for fear that the rope would slip after all. Finally I heard a shout of relief. Then the rope went slack. A moment later the frog-man came bounding through the curtain of leaves. To my surprise, he had to be at least seven feet tall!

"Thanks, thanks, and many thanks!" he croaked, taking me by the waist and lifting me into the air. "Urbang Garglack thanks this boy most sincerely!"

Then his eyes grew bigger. I don't mean that he widened them. They literally got *bigger*, as if he was a man-sized version of one of those toys you squeeze in the middle to make the eyes bulge out. He dropped me and stepped back, looked me up and down, then shook his head in wonder.

"Where are you from?" he asked at last, sounding nearly

as frightened as he had when he was stuck in the mud. "Who in the world has skin like that? Or clothing like that?"

I was looking him over at the same time and wanted to say "Well, who in the world has skin like yours?" But it seemed likely that since I was in his world, the answer might well be "Everyone!"

As far as clothing, to my relief Urbang Garglack was at least wearing *something*, a fact that had not been at all clear when he was stuck in the riverbed. But whatever he had on was so coated with mud it was hard to see what it looked like. All I could really tell was that it ended shortly above his knees.

I realized something odd about his phrase "skin like that." It implied he was not surprised by my human appearance, just the color of my skin.

"Do you have people like me on this world?" I asked.

He rolled those enormous eyes. "Certainly we have Land People. But the proper color for Land People is blue! So where are you from? Wait! Do not answer yet. I need to rinse off!"

He turned and bounded toward the river.

"Aren't you afraid you'll get stuck again?" I cried.

"I'll be more careful this time. With the water disappearing, I didn't think there would be any left underground to make sucky-sand. Big mistake! I should have known better!" With that, he disappeared through the leaves.

I moved forward and parted some branches to watch. He raced lightly across the mud, swiveling his head right and left as if constantly scanning the ground. When he came to the banks of dead fish he dropped down, then made a breathtaking leap that carried him high over that gross barrier. Once he reached what was left of the river he plunged in and sank beneath the surface. I wondered if I would ever see him again. Maybe he would use the chance to get away from me, since my appearance had clearly disturbed him.

He splashed around for a while. Several times he submerged completely, staying under so long that I wondered if he had drowned, or maybe made an underwater getaway. But each time he eventually surfaced. Finally he started back, dripping but considerably cleaner. Whatever he was wearing was still mud-stained but at least it was no longer coated with a thick layer of the stuff.

"Better," he said when he had stepped through the leaves and into the clear space. "Now talk."

I hesitated. Was it all right to tell him my story? It seemed dangerous, somehow. But I was alone in a new world, and I had just saved his life, and I definitely needed some guidance. Stalling for time, I said, "What do you want to know, Urbang Garglack?"

"Where are you from? Why are you here? Also, please call me just Urbang."

I decided to risk it and simply tell him my story. "My name is Hurricane," I began.

His eyes grew wider as he listened, though they didn't actually bulge out again. I'm sure he would have found what I said impossible to believe, if not for two things. The first was simple: since he had never seen anyone who looked quite like me, it was easy enough to believe I had come from another world. The second was more disturbing. When I had finished my tale, he said, "That sounds sadly like what is happening here."

Given the dying river, it was easy enough to guess what he meant, but to be certain, I asked, "Are you losing your water?"

He nodded, his broad, froglike face grave. "Our water is disappearing, just as your wind did. If it does not come back soon everything will die. I should be at . . . well, I should be somewhere. But I was visiting my sister and her taddlers when it began."

"What are taddlers?"

He smiled, which made it look as if his head might split in half. "When our children start to grow legs so they can walk around, we call them taddlers."

That made me smile, too. "So where are you going now?" I asked.

"Can't talk about it. It's secret."

Before I could say anything else his eyes did that bulging thing again. At the same time, he yanked my arm and whispered, "Behind the tree! Quick and quiet!"

I had no idea what had upset him, but I didn't resist. It was his world, after all. We crouched against the tree. In another moment I heard a jangling sound. A moment after that a husky voice said, "I tell you, they're in here!"

A sudden shaft of light let me know that someone had pulled apart the branches on the side of the tree that faced the road.

Without a word, Urbang bounded through the branches, back to the riverbed. I cursed him for abandoning me and crouched lower. If I was lucky, whoever had just come through the branches would go after the frogman and ignore me.

I was not lucky. "There were two of them," said a different voice. "Go on in and look."

I tried to scoot around the tree, hoping to keep the trunk between me and whoever came in. It didn't work. As I shifted to avoid the intruder, I was instantly spotted by the one still standing at the edge of the branches. Except for the fact that he was blue as a summer sky, he was clearly human—or, as Urbang would put it, a Land Person. Given the helmet and leather breastplate he wore, not to mention the sword at his side, I guessed he was a soldier . . . or maybe a cop. Did they have cops here?

The blue man shouted. I turned and ran, which brought me smack into the grip of the first guy who had come under the branches. He wrapped his arms around me and lifted me from the ground. I struggled and squirmed, trying to break free, but he was very tall, soldier-strong, and well protected from my flailing feet by his armor.

"What in the world have you caught?" said the second man. "Look at those clothes . . . and that skin!"

"Some demon friend of the witch's, I'd wager," said the one holding me.

"I don't know any witches!" I shouted.

The second soldier snorted, then said, "Into the wagon with him."

As my captor dragged me from under the tree, my heart sank. At least twenty soldiers were waiting on the road. They were mounted on the strangest-looking creatures I had ever seen: six-legged animals shorter than horses, though not so low that their riders' feet would drag on the ground. Their ears drooped past their shoulders, and their long snouts were almost like those of an anteater. Each animal was a solid color, vivid and bright as a starter set of crayons. They were lined up two by two, and except for a pair midway along the column all had saddles and bridles. The two exceptions were harnessed to an enclosed wagon. My captor dragged me toward it.

"What have I done?" I demanded, still squirming.

"We saw you with one of the Mud People," said his comrade. "Isn't that enough?"

"I just met him! He was stuck in the mud and I saved him!"

"All the more reason to arrest you," snorted the man holding me. Then, talking past me, he shouted, "Open the wagon. And be careful not to let the witch escape!"

Great. Not only was I a captive, but I was about to be tossed into a rolling cell along with a witch. Somehow it seemed likely that in this world witches were real. So I hoped she wouldn't be in a mood to turn me into a frog. Or a frog-man.

As one soldier opened the door and the other shoved me in, I realized one more thing. I no longer had my pack.

9

LURA

It was dark inside the wagon, the only light coming from a barred window in the door through which I had just been tossed. It took a moment for my eyes to adjust to the gloom. When they did I saw a girl leaning against one wall. If this was the witch the soldiers had been talking about, she sure wasn't what I had expected.

To begin with, she wasn't an old hag. Other than the fact that her skin was robin's-egg blue, she could have been in my class at school. She wore a white tunic and leather sandals with crisscrossing straps that came nearly up to her knees. A black cloak with red lining hung from her shoulders. Her sapphire hair tumbled nearly to her waist.

"Who are you?" she snapped. Looking at me more closely, she added, "And where are you from?"

I couldn't tell whether she was angry or scared. Both, probably. But from the way she tensed her body—I had seen that look on the street often enough—she wanted to cut and run.

Except there was nowhere to go.

The wagon lurched into motion and I cried out as I felt a sharp twist in my gut. As if it wasn't bad enough that I was a prisoner, my captors were taking me the wrong way . . . away from the hornpath!

The girl looked at me in concern. "Are you all right?"

"No," I said, not bothering to lie. I felt sick to the bottom of my soul.

As if she was responding to my distress, I could sense her trying to pull herself together. Clearly working to keep her voice under control, she repeated, "Where are you from? What are you doing here?"

Figuring that at this point I had nothing to lose, I told her everything I had just told Urbang. When I was done she stayed silent for several minutes. Finally she asked, "So the wind on your world has stopped completely?"

"Yep. And it seems like I'm the only one who can do anything about it. Which is totally crazy. But you can see that I'm definitely not from your world. So doesn't that kind of prove I'm telling the truth?"

She made a face. "You could be telling the truth. Or it could be that Solarian has put you here to try to get a confession out of me."

"Who is Solarian?"

"The king, and don't try to pretend you don't know that!"

I rolled my eyes. "What do you think? I'm secretly blue

and wearing makeup to fool you?" I held out my arm. "Go ahead, try to rub some off. The skin you see is what I was born with."

She scowled but then, very slowly, approached. As she was stretching a finger toward my arm the wagon jounced and she fell against me. We quickly pulled apart. I saw that her cheeks had turned a darker shade of blue, which I figured meant she was blushing. I realized my own cheeks were burning, too.

"Sorry," I said, as if it was somehow my fault, not the wagon's.

"Never mind," she replied sharply. Darting forward, she ran her thumb roughly over my cheek, then pulled it away and looked at it.

"You are not wearing paint," she said, sounding amazed, troubled, and relieved all at the same time.

"Yep. What you see is all me."

"So you really are from another world?"

"Yes. And I'm starting to feel pretty sure that what happened to my world must be connected to what's happening here. Can you tell me more about it? I learned some from Urbang, but he ran off when—"

"Urbang? You talked to one of the Water People?"

"If you mean a froggy-looking guy with big eyes, then yes. But the soldiers called him a Mud Person, not a Water Person."

The blue girl made a disgusted face. "That is a rude and insulting term. My mother taught me more respect for the

Water People than that. Also, this Urbang you met was not a 'guy.' Among the Water People, Urbang is strictly a female name."

Oops! I was glad I hadn't called Urbang a guy to her face! But, seriously, how was I supposed to figure that out? Nothing about her had made me think *Lady Frog Person!* But then, it's not easy to tell a boy frog from a girl frog on Earth, either. Lesson learned: When meeting a new species, don't assume *anything*!

The girl interrupted my thoughts. "What happened to her? One of the reasons I was out here was to try to find one of them."

"Well, I don't think much of this one. When the soldiers showed up she just took off, even though I had saved her life only a few minutes earlier."

"So you think she should have stayed and been captured along with you?" the girl asked, her voice sharp.

I started to say, "Of course!" but then realized that maybe she had a point. Which confused me. In the books and movies I know, you would naturally expect someone whose life you'd saved to stick by you. But what good would it have done if Urbang and I had both been captured? It hit me that though the translation magic let me speak to people here, that didn't mean it would let me *understand* them.

"Why were you looking for one of these Water People?" I asked, partly to change the subject.

"I would rather not say!" she snapped. Then she slid to

the floor, settled back against the wagon wall, and closed her eyes.

I had no idea if this was a natural response on her world, or if she was just annoyed. I positioned myself against the opposite wall and glared at her. Given that she had her eyes closed, this was not very effective.

The cart continued to jounce along. The jolting movement started to get to me, and I thought, *People who can build towers like the ones I saw ought to be able to do a better job on their roads.* Then I thought about some of the back roads around where Mom and I had lived before we moved to Chi-town and realized that for all I knew these people did have superhighways somewhere else. Then I thought, *Well, if they have superhighways, why do they ride these weird not-quite-horses?* And then I thought about the fact that people on Earth still ride horses, and if you were going to go out on a road like this, maybe horseback would be the best way to do it.

This going-to-a-different-world thing was confusing.

"Hey, um, girl . . . you asleep?" I asked after a while.

The blue girl opened one eye. "No. And my name is Lura."

"What do you call those horsey things the soldiers are riding?"

"Horses," she said, looking at me as if I was an idiot.

Which made me think the language thingy must be doing the best it could with what it had.

We continued to jounce along. Despite the thin layer of

straw on the floor, my butt was getting sore. But that was nothing like the pain in my heart, which grew sharper with each mile we went in the wrong direction. Through the barred window I could tell it was getting dark. Finally the wagon stopped and someone began shouting commands for the men to make camp. I got to my feet and looked out. We had left the road and were now in a clearing in a wooded area.

Lura opened her eyes and said, "I wonder if they'll feed us."

"Don't prisoners usually get fed?" I asked.

She shrugged, which seemed to mean the same thing here that it does on Earth. "Usually. But I'm not a usual prisoner."

"Why not? And why are you a prisoner anyway? They called you a witch before they threw me in here. But you don't seem like a witch."

"That's because I'm not a witch." She was silent for a moment, then said, "I'm the goddess of water."

I nearly snorted but managed to hold it in.

"Go ahead and laugh! It's as ridiculous as it sounds. There is a god of water, but it's certainly not me."

"Is that why you're a prisoner, for impersonating a goddess?"

"No! This sacrilege was the king's idea. And I'm not even the first. It started with my mother."

"So why are you a prisoner?" I repeated.

"Because I ran away."

"Because everyone blamed you for the problem with the water and you thought they were going to kill you?"

"You're half-right. They are indeed blaming me, and I'm sure my life was in danger. But the real reason I left was to seek Belaquian, the *true* god of water. I want to beg his forgiveness and plead for his aid. I thought it was possible a Water Person might help me find the way."

I blinked at her. "Your gods are still hanging around where people can find them?"

Lura sniffed. "The god of water does not 'hang around,' whatever that means. It was another god altogether who was hung. I know of Belaquian only through tales my mother told me, stories from the days before Solarian became king. Belaquian was the patron and protector of all humankind. He crafted a fountain, which he called Worldwater, then primed it with his own blood. From the fountain flowed the water that filled the streams and rivers, then the lakes and eventually the oceans." She paused, then added, "At least, that is what my mother believed. Many stories tell of his home in the cliffs at the headwaters of the River Sar. But now that river is dying. If there really is a Belaquian, I must find him and beseech him to have mercy on my people."

A haunted look came into her eyes. "The idea of doing this fills me with fear. His fury with me must be great."

"Why?"

"You really are from another world, aren't you? When Solarian seized the crown, he forbade the worship of the

Bringer of Waters. Belaquian's statue, which had stood for centuries in front of the Temple of Water, was pulled down and destroyed. Then Solarian placed my mother, who had been high priestess in the temple, on the Throne of Waters and proclaimed her the new goddess of water."

"I don't get it," I said. "What was the point of all that?"

"Power. And money. Solarian controlled my mother, and then me. We were forced to issue whatever proclamations he ordered. Oddly, most of the things he had us proclaim put money in the royal treasury. I fear Belaquian has finally decided to punish us all for this blasphemy and that is why he has stilled the fountain. I have to make him understand that it was the king who turned away, not the people. Then he will forgive us."

"And you believe all this?"

Lura scowled. "I don't know what to think. It seems unlikely. Yet when my mother spoke of Belaquian something in her voice, something about the stories, made them feel true. And the night she died she made me promise to find Belaquian and beg his forgiveness." Lura closed her eyes and whispered, "It's been a year since then. A year since the king proclaimed me goddess. I should have tried to escape right away. But I was fearful of the king . . . and closely guarded by the temple priests. Now I am more fearful of what will happen if I *don't* find Belaquian—what will happen if the water never comes back."

I thought of my own mother, struggling for breath in that clinic, and knew I couldn't say anything about Lura's mother without starting to cry. And I feared that if I did start, I might never stop.

It had grown full dark while we talked. Though the smell of roasting meat drifted in to tease our nostrils, it turned out Lura had been right—no one brought us food.

After it became clear we weren't going to be fed, we settled down to sleep. Well, we tried to. Personally, I had no luck. My stomach was sending me angry messages. The straw was itchy. I couldn't stop wondering what had happened to Zephron. And the fact that we were heading in the wrong direction created a constant, nagging ache inside me.

It didn't help that I could still hear the soldiers talking.

"What do you suppose the king will do with the traitor goddess?" asked one.

"Burn her in the public square, I'd wager," answered another.

"Probably her demon along with her," said a third, sounding all too happy at the idea.

The "demon" was me! Not the kind of words to soothe you into slumber . . . which was why I was still awake when something rattled at the wagon door.

A flash of hope lifted my heart. Had Zephron managed to reach this world after all? Had he somehow tracked me down?

I touched Lura's arm.

"I'm awake," she whispered.

At her voice, a sudden fear replaced my hope. What if

the rattling at the door was one of the soldiers, someone who had decided to take action on his own and punish the witch and her "demon" for the missing water?

That was the last thought on my mind as the door swung open.

WILD RIDE

Standing at the entrance to the wagon was Urbang Garglack. As I breathed a sigh of relief, the frog-woman held up a wide, webbed hand to caution me to silence.

"I thought you had run away," I whispered, scrambling to my feet.

Urbang rolled her enormous eyes. "What good could I have done you had I been captured? Escape and then come back later to help is smarter."

Looking past me, she spotted Lura. She hesitated, then nodded, as if she had decided something. Voice low but urgent, she said, "You two go to the horses. I will create a diversion. When the guard comes to investigate my disturbance, untie the horses . . . *all* of them! Then mount up and ride for your lives. I'll catch up later."

I felt a surge of panic. "But I . . ."

Urbang was gone before the rest of my sentence dropped into the night air.

". . . never rode a horse before."

Lura looked at me in astonishment. "What a strange world you come from," she whispered. "Well, follow me. I'll get you out of here."

"I'll make it," I hissed.

We crept out of the wagon. The fires had burned low, but each fire pit still gave off a small glow. A single soldier stood guard. I looked around and was relieved to spot my pack leaning against the front of the wagon. I nudged Lura and pointed it out to her, then dropped to the ground, crawled to the pack, and slipped it on. As I did, I heard a rustle in the bushes on the far side of the camp.

The guard clearly heard it, too—I saw him turn to look.

The bushes rustled again.

"Who goes there?" demanded the guard.

The rustling continued.

The guard put his hand on the hilt of his sword. As he did the sound stopped. "Just some animal," he muttered, relaxing again.

Then a loud sneeze sounded from the bushes. The guard drew his sword and dashed toward it.

Bending low, Lura and I raced for the strange, low-slung, candy-colored "horses." Quickly we began undoing the ropes that held them to the makeshift hitching rail the soldiers had put up.

Things were silent on the far side of the camp. I hoped that meant Urbang had managed to overcome the guard.

When we had the horses untied Lura leaned close to me and said, "Mount up."

"Without a saddle?"

"No time for that! Pick a horse, climb on, then grab his mane and lock your knees to his sides."

"How do I steer him?"

"He'll follow me. Trust me."

The beasts were so low to the ground that all it took was a small hop for me to fling a leg over the back of the nearest "horse," which happened to be yellow. When Lura saw that I was safely mounted, she began riding back and forth behind the rest of the horses, shouting as she lashed at them with one of the ropes that had been used to tie them. I thought making all that noise was crazy, then realized that scattering the horses would keep the soldiers from following us.

The horses broke into a run. The one I was riding joined in, shooting forward like a rocket. I bounced sideways, nearly fell off, then managed to pull myself back up. Remembering Lura's instructions, I locked my knees to its sides, grabbed its mane, and held on for dear life.

Behind us the camp erupted into action. The men were shouting in rage, but what could they do? The horses had a big head start and were moving faster than anyone on foot could ever manage.

From the corner of my eye I saw Urbang leaping through the trees. I thought she might jump onto one of the horses. Instead she continued to hop along beside us, covering huge distances with every bounce.

As for me, I was clinging to my horse with every ounce of strength I possessed. Between being so low-slung and having six legs, the beasts did not gallop the way I'd seen horses do in movies. Instead, they made a kind of hunching movement, like giant caterpillars moving at high speed. And I do mean high speed. This thing was blazing along, with me bouncing from side to side as it veered wildly through the darkness. It had to veer like that, since you can't gallop through a forest in a straight line. Even so, the zigs and zags made it hard to keep my grip, despite the fact that I had my knees locked like a vise against my mount's sides.

We came to a narrow ditch, probably a place that had once been a stream feeding into the river. Without breaking stride, my horse sailed across. I hadn't been prepared for the leap—or the jolt of the landing—and slipped far to the left, barely managing to keep from falling off. This meant nothing to the creature and it hurtled on. My strength doubled by the fear of death, I tried to pull myself back to an upright position. The rest of the stampede was catching up. If I fell now I would be cut to ribbons by their slashing hooves.

Suddenly a monstrous orange horse with eyes like fire thundered up beside us. The sight of it gave me a burst of adrenaline and with a last, desperate lunge I pulled myself back to an upright position.

"Well done!" shouted Urbang.

Moments later we broke out of the woods and back onto the road. And still we raced onward. Leaning low across the animal's neck, I redoubled my grip on its mane. My legs were locked against its sides so tightly that my thighs throbbed with pain.

All at once Lura was beside me, riding in a crouch, a grim smile on her face, her cloak streaming out behind her. I caught her pose, imitated it, and began to feel more at ease.

Then I flashed her a smile to prove I wasn't worried.

After a while our pace slowed, first to a trot, finally to a walk.

"Were you trying get me killed?" I asked, once I had caught my breath.

"Just get you out of there alive."

"I wasn't entirely sure that was going to happen."

"But it did."

She had a point. "Thanks," I said. "You, too, Urbang. Oh—you haven't met Lura!"

"Not met," Urbang said. "But I know well who she is."

"How do you know that?" Lura asked.

Urbang goggled her eyes. "I know you because Belaquian showed us your image in his viewing pool many times over the last year."

"You know Belaquian?" Lura cried.

"I most certainly do! My family has been in his service for generations."

Lura looked nervous. "He must be so angry with us that he has stopped up the waters to punish us for not believing!"

"I do not think that is so," said Urbang.

"Why not?"

"It is not his way. Oh, he was indeed angry about what your king did with the statue and the temple, but he also seemed amused. I think he considered it in the line of 'silly human tricks.' He has said more than once that he thought the world was outgrowing him and it might be time for him to move on."

While the two of them were talking, I felt a tug at my heart and realized something wonderful. I had caught the sense of the horn again. I was so distracted by this, I lost track of the conversation for a moment. When I tuned in again, I heard Urbang say, "Whatever the reason the water is disappearing, it isn't because Belaquian turned it off. Something far worse has happened."

"How do you know all this?" I asked.

"I am one of Belaquian's most trusted servants."

"So you know the way to his home?" Lura asked eagerly.

"His home is my home. That is where I was heading when Hurricane rescued me from the sucky-sand. I had gone to visit my sister but had cut the visit short and was heading back to the Cavern of Waters because I knew something had gone horribly wrong. That is where I am going now."

"Take me with you!" said Lura.

Urbang did a major eye-goggle. "It is a secret and sacred place!"

"You and I were already traveling that way," I said. "And I would be surprised if the trail I follow doesn't lead me there anyway. So I think we should stay together."

The corners of Urbang's wide mouth turned down. "I sense a deep mystery in all this. But you are correct, Hurricane. As we are indeed heading in the same direction it would be foolish to separate now." She glanced behind us. "Foolish, as well, to stay still too long. The rest of the horses, being riderless, will return to the camp. Once they do, the soldiers might come after us again. We need to get off the road. We'll be too easy to spot here."

We directed our mounts to push through the outer curtain of the trees that lined the river. Well, Lura directed her horse. Mine simply trailed along. Urbang continued to hop beside us. I noticed that the other horses didn't follow.

This diversion was difficult for me, because we were leaving the direct path. But I could still sense the horn's trail off to our side, so I didn't panic. It was pitch black under the canopy of trees so I took out my lantern and said, "Light."

"Impressive," said Urbang when the lantern began to glow. "And useful. We should stay under the trees for as long as we can. We'll be too easy to spot on the road."

As we traveled, I explained in more detail what had happened on Earth. Lura interrupted frequently to question parts of my story and fill in parts of her own. When I was done, she said, "Your tale may be even stranger than mine. But it does give me hope that we might find Belaquian. Is he not something like this Zephron of yours?"

"Sounds like he might be," I said. "Only maybe even more powerful. The fact that the two of them seemed to have something in common was one of the reasons I was able to believe your story."

After a time we came to the end of the tree tunnel and had to use the road again. It was a bit riskier, but easier on my heart to be connected directly to the trail. As we passed from beneath the trees I saw that the moon—yellowish and larger than the one I was used to—had drifted into the sky. Its light was strong enough that I was able to put away the lantern.

Awhile later another moon, smaller and distinctly green, followed the first into the sky. The sight gave me a chill. I was so far from home! The stars were different, too. I didn't know many constellations . . . you don't see much of the stars in a city like Chicago. But I knew the Big Dipper, and it was strange not to be able to find it.

The road continued along the side of the riverbed, through open territory now. I had no way to keep track of time, so I don't know how long it was before we reached the forest, which grew right to the edge of the muddy bank. The first line of trees, straight and huge, stood like a row of guards. I had to tip my head so far back to see their tops that it hurt my neck.

Lura reached over and took my arm. "This is Dredmor Wood," she said softly. "It's haunted."

Urbang began to laugh.

THE TRAP

"What's so funny?" Lura demanded, glaring at Urbang.

The frog-woman smiled that face-splitting smile. "The forest is not haunted. However, we Water Folk wanted the Land People to believe that it is. So we created the stories ourselves, then got them to circulate among the Landsters."

"Why?" I asked.

Urbang shrugged. "It reduces intruders."

"Haunted or not, I still think we should wait till morning to go in," Lura said. "Even if there aren't strange creatures living in there, it will be very dark. Let's sleep here and begin again in the morning."

"No, no," said Urbang. "Far better to sleep in the woods. Even if some horses get back to the camp and the soldiers ride this way, they will not come into the 'haunted' forest."

"I agree with Urbang," I said.

Lura scowled but nodded.

"You should let your horses go now," said Urbang. "Dredmor Wood is too dense for riding."

I had grown almost fond of the strange yellow creature I had been riding. Reluctantly, I slid to the ground, then almost fell flat. My legs were shaky and achy!

Following Lura's lead, I slapped Lemon (yes, I had named him in my head) on the rump. The two beasts, one yellow, the other bright purple, sped into action, hunching back along the road like a pair of giant six-legged caterpillars.

When we had walked about a hundred yards into the forest we came to an open area big enough to let us make some camp beds. To my surprise, Urbang said, "I will leave you for the night."

"Where are you going?" I asked, startled at how unhappy this announcement made me.

"Out to the riverbed. I need to get back into the water for what is left of the night. I will rejoin you in the morning."

As we watched her hop away Lura said, "Do you think she's up to some kind of mischief?"

"Why would I think that?"

Lura shook her head. "The Land People and the Water Folk have long been enemies. My mother taught me to think differently, but I can't entirely forget other stories I have heard. I'm not entirely comfortable with Urbang."

At the moment, I had a different uncomfortable feeling:

hunger! The excitement of that wild horseback ride had pushed all thoughts of eating aside. Now that we were finally in a place that seemed safe and we could relax a bit, my stomach announced in no uncertain terms that it expected to be fed . . . and soon!

Thank goodness I had retrieved my pack. I just about tore the thing open.

"What are you after?" asked Lura when she saw my hurry.

"I've got some food in here!"

She smiled and said, "I hereby take back any bad thoughts I have had about you."

I took out some of the provisions I had packed back in Zephron's cave and shared them with her.

"Good," she said.

My own thought was that the stuff was *amazingly* good. How could dried meat and dried fruit be so light and chewy and flavorful?

Once we had eaten, we gathered leaves and made camp beds. The night had grown cool and I took the blanket out of my pack. It was thin, which was good because that meant it didn't take up much space, but it also made me wonder how warm it would be. I shouldn't have been surprised to discover that the answer was "very warm indeed."

I glanced over at Lura. "You going to be warm enough?"

"One reason I wore this cloak is that it also makes an excellent blanket," she replied. Which I took to mean "Yes."

Exhaustion has its uses, and I slept better than I had expected.

I dreamed of my mother.

In the morning I handed Lura some more food from my pack. Rather than fight through the mud and dead fish to drink from what was left of the river, we shared some of the water still left in my canteen. Just as I was beginning to feel itchy about getting started for the day, Urbang came leaping back into the clearing. "Sleep well?" she asked. "I did. The mud was quite pleasant after that long, dry walk. Not *enough* sleep, though. We turned in way too late for that. Still, best we get going."

I rolled my blanket and stuffed it into my pack, and we set off.

The forest was dense, the branches shutting out almost all the light. The leaves rustled beneath our feet. An unexpected breeze almost set me to dancing.

The trail of the horn stayed close to the riverbed. Urbang was content to let me lead the way, saying, "So far this is exactly the path I would be following anyway."

Which made me more certain than ever that the horn had been taken to the cavern where she claimed Belaquian lived.

Sometimes we walked right along the muddy bank. More than once when we were doing so I glanced at Lura and saw tears streaming down her blue cheeks as she gazed at the pathetic remainder of what had been a great waterway.

On the far side of that wide depression was more forest. It grew right to the edge of the mud, so thick it was impossible to see into it.

Through the day my sense of the horn grew ever more intense. I was constantly on the edge of breaking into a run, and several times Lura and Urbang had to ask me to slow my pace. We stopped twice to rest and eat, though doing so was painful. The call of the horn had a tight hold on me now.

Late in the morning of our second day, the forest gloom began to lift. As the way ahead grew brighter we quickened our pace. Soon we came to the edge of the woods . . . where we halted in dismay.

Urbang groaned and said, "It's worse than I had feared."

We were standing at the top of a cliff. It wasn't that high, really . . . maybe twenty-five feet. Still, it was too far down for us to jump. But that wasn't the main problem. At the base of the cliff, and stretching on for miles, was what had once been a large lake. Now it was a vast plain of mud and muck, strewn with drying weeds and dying fish. Even from where we stood the stench of the fish was powerful. At the center of the former lake remained a small circle of water, little more than a pond.

"The water used to come to within an arm's length of where we stand," said Urbang sadly.

As if to prove her point, to our right I saw a boat that was tied to a tree. Only instead of floating on water, the boat now dangled from the rope, its bottom bumping against the side of the cliff.

Crossing this mess was going to be difficult—not to mention disgusting. And what was on the far side was even more forbidding: the enormous cliffs that cupped the end of the valley. The walls of stone seemed to stretch straight into the sky, disappearing at last into a bank of heavy clouds. The rock was black. From where we stood, it seemed as smooth as glass.

I wish Shamoondra was here, I thought. *Then we could just fly over all that mud!*

The smooth face of the cliffs was broken by a line that ran unevenly down the center. Shielding my eyes from the sun, I made out that it was a waterfall. It must have been the source of the Sar. It had probably been a thundering torrent at one time. Now it was just a wavering silver thread. To my surprise, it didn't fall from the top of the cliffs. Instead it came from somewhere in the middle of them, appearing to spring out of solid rock.

I felt uneasy, fearful of whatever was hidden inside those cliffs. I glanced at Lura. She was trembling but it wasn't from fear. The expression on her face was pure longing. "We're wasting time," she cried, heading for the edge of the cliff. "Let's go!"

Despite my discomfort about what lay ahead, the call of the horn was too strong to resist. Urbang and I caught up to Lura. We stopped at the edge, looking down. The face of the cliff was sheer and smooth, with nothing to offer a handhold or foothold. I looked right and left, thinking maybe we could find another spot from which to climb down. But not more than ten feet in either direction the rock walls grew even higher and were equally sheer. I didn't want to backtrack, and not just because we would lose time. I was afraid of losing the trail completely.

I shucked my pack, took out the coil of rope, then tied it around the tree closest to the edge of the cliff.

Lura looked at it dubiously. "Will that be long enough?"

Urbang chuckled. "Based on what happened when Hurricane helped me escape the sucky-sand, it will be as long as it needs to be."

We dropped the free end of the rope over the edge of the cliff.

Sure enough, it made it to the bottom.

"I'll go first," said Lura, so eager to get moving that it was almost as if she was feeling the same pull I did.

She grasped the rope and went backward over the edge. I had seen this in enough movies that I figured I knew what do, so after giving her time to get a little way down, I slipped my pack back on, then followed.

Going down that way wasn't as easy as it looked. The rope was rough against my hands, and I had to hold on tight to keep from just sliding down—which would have caused a major rope burn. Still, I was doing all right. The first sign of trouble was a shout from Lura that got cut off. I twisted to look over my shoulder but couldn't see her.

Worried, I tried to speed up. Without warning, a strange humming filled my ears and the world went black. I felt a moment of breathtaking cold, then found myself in a . . . well, a room.

A room shaped like an egg.

A really, really big egg.

And it didn't have any door, at least not one that I could see.

Lura was beside me, looking baffled and terrified.

"What is this place?" I whispered.

"How would I know?" she snapped.

I would have been angry, but I realized it had been a stupid question. Before I could say anything else, Urbang arrived. Just . . . arrived. We didn't see her enter. She simply wasn't there, and then she was.

"What is this place?" I asked again.

Urbang looked around for a moment, then said, "It would appear we've fallen into a trap."

"A trap?" I said. "Well, how do we get out?"

Urbang rolled her huge eyes in what was becoming an annoyingly familiar gesture. "We just got *in*. Give me a moment to examine the place, will you? I'm not sure we *can* get out."

"So what do we do?" I demanded.

"We be quiet so we can think!"

I took the message . . . and took a deep breath, trying to calm myself.

Silently the three of us examined the gray space that enclosed us. It was about twelve feet long, and the rounded wall—there were no corners, so it really was just one curving wall—tapered down at either end. One end was fairly pointy, the other more blunt. A slice through the center, which was where we stood, would be a perfect circle about eight feet across. It was barely high enough for Urbang to stand upright.

I took the knife from my pack and tried to push it into the side closest to me. The wall stretched, but the blade could not penetrate it. I dropped the knife and pushed with my hands instead. The wall bent under the pressure and I was able to stretch it much farther than the knife had. But though the wall bent, it didn't break . . . and as soon as I dropped my hands, it sprang back into place without even showing a mark.

"Let's try together," said Lura.

"Perhaps at one of the ends," suggested Urbang. "They might be the weak spots."

We gathered shoulder to shoulder at the blunt end of our prison and began to push. The gray wall stretched out a foot, then two, then three. But it felt no thinner and reached a point where it would go no farther, no matter how hard we pushed. As soon as we stepped away it sprang back, again showing no sign at all that it had been stretched. Furious, I kicked it. My foot bounced back so fast it nearly knocked me over.

"Well, clearly *that's* not going to work," said Urbang. She went to the center of our prison, sat down cross-legged, then laid her webbed hands on her knees. She closed her eyes. A peaceful expression settled over her face. Then her throat bulged out and she began to make a low but powerful thrumming.

It was my turn to roll my eyes, but Lura put a hand on my arm and I managed to keep myself from saying anything stupid.

I thought Urbang's thrumming was getting louder, then realized what was actually going on. Somehow the sound was being held in by the wall, so that it was building up inside the egg. None of it was fading away and it gained volume until it was painful. I was about to beg Urbang to stop when the wall began to shimmer.

"That's it!" I cried. "You're getting it! Keep going!"

Lura tugged at my sleeve and shook her head to indicate I should not interrupt what Urbang was doing. Lura was right, and I felt foolish. It's just that where I come from we like to cheer people on.

The closest part of the wall looked thinner now. I poked at it and it yielded to my finger far more easily than before.

"Lura," I whispered. "Help me push!"

She moved to my side and we pressed as hard as we could. Urbang's thrumming pounded in my skull. But the wall was giving, stretching and thinning beneath our hands like a balloon. Just a little more, I was sure, and it would burst. Sweat ran into my eyes. It stung, but I didn't dare release the pressure on the wall.

Then Urbang stopped thrumming. At once, the wall snapped back into position, knocking Lura and me to the floor.

INTO THE FLOW

"Why did you stop?" I cried. "And what were you doing, anyway?"

"I was using the Thrum of Dissolution. It was starting to work, but I'm not strong enough to do it myself." Urbang's voice was calm but I could see that she was trembling from the effort she had put out. I also saw a glint of anger in her huge eyes.

"Well, it was a good try," I said.

"Thank you. But good is not good enough."

"Would it help if we went into the Flow?" Lura asked.

"What's the Flow?" I asked. At the same moment Urbang, clearly startled and sounding a bit angry, said, "How do *you* know about the Flow?"

Lura blinked and took a step back. "My mother taught me."

Urbang scowled. "The Flow is a Water People thing. How in the world would your mother know about it?"

"She told me she learned it from Belaquian."

At this Urbang goggled her eyes.

"Mind telling me what this is all about?" I asked impatiently.

"Entering the Flow is a way of joining minds together to use their combined power," Urbang explained.

"And how do you do that?"

"We lower our barriers and let our minds flow as if they are merging streams, moving to the great ocean of mind and spirit that connects all being. It comes naturally to Water People, though we do have to be trained to it. I have never known of a Land Person who could do it."

"Well, I can," Lura insisted. "And if you think that whatever you were doing to break through those walls could be made stronger by me joining with you, then we should try."

"Yes, yes, you are right," said Urbang. "Well, come and sit with me."

Lura did as Urbang asked, positioning herself so that their knees were almost touching. They closed their eyes and sat in silence for a while. I stood by, feeling both mystified and left out.

After a few minutes Urbang began to thrum again. The sound went on longer this time and grew so loud I had to cover my ears. I could see the wall getting thinner. I started to push against it and managed to stretch it farther than ever. But just as I was sure that this time we were going to break out, Urbang stopped.

Instantly the wall snapped back to its regular shape and size.

"Why did you stop?" I cried.

"Because it wasn't going to work."

"But you almost had it!"

"It wasn't going to work," repeated Urbang.

I thought for a minute, then said, "Would it help if I joined in? Could you teach me to do it?"

Urbang looked uneasy, but Lura said, "It won't hurt to try. We'll need to rest first, though. We just poured out a lot of energy."

With that, she and Urbang lay flat on their backs and closed their eyes. I couldn't believe it! I wanted to get out of this place as fast as possible and they were going to take a nap? I mean, I understood them being tired. But I wasn't tired, I was wired.

I circled around them, poking at the gray wall, until Lura opened one eye and said, "Hurricane, if you don't sit down and let us rest, we'll never get out of this place."

I sat. I stewed. I fumed. I fussed.

But I did it all quietly. After a while I heard Mom's voice in my head, saying what she always said when I was getting impatient: "Hurricane, I have known many strong and brilliant people, and not one of them was able to make time pass faster just because they wanted it to."

Right again, Mom, I thought. Which somehow made me feel better.

I slid along the floor to the broad end of the egg. Turned out the curve in the wall at that spot was pretty comfortable. I dug my fingers into the wall and discovered I could grasp a chunk of it and squeeze, then release, then squeeze again. I diverted my restless energy to that.

Finally Urbang sat up. A moment later Lura did, too.

"All right," said the frog-woman. "Let's give it a try. Hurricane, come sit with us."

I wanted to say, "It's about freaking time!" but bit back the words. I knew they wanted to get out of here as much as I did. I walked over and took my place beside them.

"Now join hands," Urbang said.

I took Lura's hand, thinking how odd it was to see her blue fingers tangled in mine. Then I took Urbang's hand. It was not slimy, as I had expected, just very smooth and cool. Because her webbing made it impossible to interlock fingers, Urbang just closed her hand—which was very large—over mine.

"I think I should start," Lura said. "It might be easier for me to reach Hurricane."

"I agree," Urbang said. "After all, you are both Land Folk."

"What are you going to do?" I asked, feeling uneasy.

"I'll be trying to reach you with my mind," Lura said. "But for that to work, you'll need to relax and drop your mental barriers."

"My what?"

"We all have barriers in our minds to protect us from

intrusion," Urbang explained. "You will have to let those barriers down, first for Lura, then for me. It won't be easy, but once you do and we meet in the Flow, the strength and force of your being can be added to ours. My hope is that with three of us combining energies I can finally break us out of here."

"Start by relaxing," Lura said.

"I always relax when I'm caught in a giant squishy egg," I muttered.

"Sarcasm will impede the Flow," said Urbang. "Relax, and trust us."

I closed my eyes and tried to relax. It wasn't easy. Years of living in the hard parts of Chicago had taught me that relaxation was dangerous.

After a while I felt a tickle in my brain. It made me shiver.

"Relax," whispered Lura. Urbang began to thrum again. This time the sound was soft and soothing. *This is how it starts, Hurricane,* said Lura. Only she didn't say it out loud. She was speaking directly into my mind!

My brain slammed up a set of walls I hadn't even known I possessed. I was trembling as if I was naked in a snowstorm. I couldn't let anyone get so close, get *inside me* like that.

Stop fighting, Lura urged. But her words were dim and distant now.

Go away! I cried . . . though not out loud.

This may be our only way out. Join with me. Join with me!

Get out of my head!!

And with that, Urbang's thrumming stopped. The power ebbed from the room. The three of us sat, looking at each other.

I felt so alone. Urbang and Lura had managed to link their minds and concentrate on trying to get us out of this trap. I was the one who hadn't been able to help.

What was I afraid of? Well, it was creepy to feel someone else in my head. And how much of my mind could Lura read while she was there? On the other hand, even if she read every single thought I had ever had, would that be as bad as being trapped in this stupid egg?

"Let's try again," I whispered.

"Lura, let me try to make the connection this time," Urbang said. "I have trained many younglings in entering the Flow."

"All right," Lura said.

"Sit facing me," said Urbang. "We'll start with just the two of us. Lura, when I nod, come join us."

I sat in front of Urbang and we joined hands again.

"Now close your eyes and listen to the sound of my breathing. Match it with your own. Slowly, slowly . . ."

I strained to catch the soft sound of her breath. Once I had the rhythm, I tried to copy it. I kept missing at first, breathing in too soon or letting go too late. But after a few minutes I had the rhythm.

"Now imagine a small stream, trickling through the forest."

I let the image form in my mind.

"Follow the stream with your eye. Ah, now, see! Another stream is flowing toward it. They merge and become a single, larger stream. Enter the water, Hurricane. Flow with the water, feel how supple and lively it is. *Be* the water. Ah, here comes yet another stream to join you."

And with that, I felt Urbang in my mind. I flinched, because the feel of her mind was so strange, so alien. Lura's mind had felt like mine, but Urbang's was . . . well, like the water she had been describing. I caught flitting images of underwater scenes—slender plants waving in a current, strangely shaped fish, other creatures for which I had no name.

Good, Urbang murmured inside my head. *Stay relaxed. Lura will join us in a moment.*

I felt Lura take my hand.

Well done, Hurricane, she thought to me.

I felt a surge of pride, then wondered if she could sense that pride, which gave me another burst of fear. What would she see here in my head?

Stay in the Flow, murmured Urbang. Then she began thrumming again.

After that, there was no time to go exploring in someone else's mind. All our strength and energy was being channeled through Urbang to break our way out of our prison.

The thrumming grew louder, more intense. The sound built up around us, so solid I could feel the pressure of it.

Then there was an explosion, and then silence.

MUD

When I opened my eyes the egg was gone. We were sitting at the foot of the cliff, at the edge of the vast bed of the former lake . . . the exact spot we had been lowering ourselves to when the trap took us.

It's not quite true that the egg was gone. Bits and pieces of gray stuff clung to the side of the cliff and were scattered for at least a hundred feet in all directions.

"Well done, us," Urbang said cheerfully. "Are you two all right?"

"I think so," I said, pushing myself to my feet. As I did I glanced at the boulder to our right. To my surprise, someone had carved a message into the side facing us. Repeating Urbang's words, it read:

WELL DONE!

"Look!" I said, pointing.

Urbang and Lura turned toward the boulder. Both of them gasped.

I hadn't been sure whether the message was written in English, or if I was only able to read it because of that crazy language thing the spheres do. Since it was clear that my companions could also read it, I decided it had to be the language spell.

"What does it mean?" Lura asked. "Who would put that there?"

"It makes no sense," Urbang replied. "Why build a trap like that, then congratulate us on escaping it?"

"Maybe whoever put it there isn't the person who built the trap?" Lura said.

"What if the trap was meant to be a test?" I suggested. "Then the congratulations would make sense."

"An interesting thought," Urbang said. "But a test for what? And placed by whom?"

For that I had no answer.

"We'll have to carry that riddle with us," Urbang said. "It's a long way across and we don't want to spend the night in . . ." She gestured to the huge expanse of mud.

My rope still dangled from the cliff. I hadn't thought about how I was going to get it back once we were all down, but when I grabbed it and gave an experimental tug, it instantly came loose from the tree to which we had tied it. By this point I wasn't even surprised. I shook the rope and it coiled into a compact loop. I returned it to my pack and we began to pick our way across the lake bed.

After a while I said, "Jeez, this is worse than moldy potato salad."

Then I wondered how Urbang and Lura would hear those words. Did they have something like potato salad in this world? If not, how would the language spell interpret it? I pulled up one foot and shook away some clinging mud. "And all these dead fish. I've never smelled anything so stomach-turning!"

I glanced at Lura. To my surprise she seemed to be ignoring the mud and the revolting smell. Instead she was gazing at the cliffs ahead with a look of longing.

"That girl is crazy," I muttered to myself.

I looked up again. The tops of the cliffs were hidden in clouds. I felt in my gut that they protected some ancient secret.

Whoever stole the horn had a lot of nerve if he took it up there, I thought. I didn't want to get near the place. But I had no choice. Wherever the horn went, I must follow.

The going got worse the farther we went into the lake bed. Dying water plants tangled around our feet, causing us to trip and stumble. In the places without plants the muck itself seemed to cling more mulishly with each step we took, except when there were big stones, which tended to be slippery instead.

To make things worse, the fish had naturally moved

toward the center as the lake shrank, which meant that the number of dead and rotting bodies grew steadily as we went on. The buzz of insects became deafening, and the dead fish shimmered blue-green under their metallic-looking bodies.

And I'm not even going to talk about the maggots.

"This isn't going to work," Urbang said at last. "We have to backtrack to where the mud is drier and circle around the center."

"But that will take so much longer!" Lura cried.

"I don't think so," said Urbang. "This muck is going to slow us down more and more, and we're still miles from the center of the lake. So the distance will be greater, but the time should be shorter." She turned to me. "Does your sense of the horn lead to the cliffs?"

I nodded and said, "We've been following it straight across. So unless the thief went down through the center of the lake when he got there, I expect it will continue on to the other side." I paused, then added, "I hate to leave the direct trail, but I agree about getting around the lake. If I can't pick up the trail on the far side we can always come back here for it."

"I am certain it will lead straight to that waterfall," Urbang said.

"Are we going to have to climb those cliffs?" I asked.

She gave me one of her head-splitting smiles and said, "You'll see when we get there. When we first started to travel together I was uncertain about bringing you to the

Cavern of Waters. But now I am convinced that both our worlds have been victims of the same thief."

I was tempted to say "What took you so long?" but managed to hold my tongue. Mom would have been proud.

"What I can't figure out," continued Urbang, "is *why*."

"That's the question I keep wondering about," said Lura.

When we diverted toward the edge of the lake I felt a stabbing pain in my heart. I should have been expecting it, but it was even worse this time than when the soldiers had taken me in the wrong direction. I hoped maybe the intensity was because we were getting closer to our goal.

Even turning away from the center of the lake, the going was a slow slog. The best we could hope for if we had to make camp was not dry land, just less-mucky muck.

Lura became increasingly agitated as we traveled. "Something," she muttered, clearly to herself and not Urbang or me. *"Something."*

Then she slipped and fell. When Urbang and I finally got her to her feet all three of us were covered with thick, clinging mud. While I was sputtering about how disgusting it was Lura cried, "Look! There's an opening!"

"Indeed there is," said Urbang calmly.

I saw it now, too. Behind the trickle of the waterfall we

had spotted from the far side of the lake yawned the black mouth of a cave.

Sundown came, but the two moons gave us enough light to carry on. That was good, because Lura and I were both desperate to keep going.

Despite the mud, and our exhaustion, we ran the last hundred yards or so to the waterfall. It was about a foot wide, though it obviously had once been much bigger. At its base glimmered a crystal-clear pool, maybe thirty feet across. From the side of the pool opposite the cliff a narrow stream, only two or three feet wide, flowed toward the center of the once-great lake.

The three of us waded into the pool and took turns standing beneath the waterfall. The cool waters sparkled silver in the moonlight and I tipped my head back to take a drink. The water was delicious, amazingly pure. Washing off the days of dirt and sweat was delicious in an entirely different way. It felt so good I didn't even mind having my clothes soaked straight through. I checked the backpack; as I suspected, it was waterproof. So I closed it up tightly, then washed that off, too.

After we had all had a turn, Lura went back and stood under the water again. Soon she started to sing. Even with the aid of the translation magic, I could not *understand* the words. Yet somehow her song made the hair on the back of my neck stand up. Was it possible there really were things that were holy? Turning to Urbang, I said, "Do we camp here for the night?"

"No, no, we must go on!" cried Lura.

"We will indeed go on," said Urbang. "The next stage of our journey will not take as long as you think. Turn on your lantern, Hurricane. I can find my way in the dark but it will be easier for you and Lura if you have light."

Once I had the lantern lit, Urbang led the way around the waterfall. The cave we entered was high and wide. To my surprise, a dozen or so boats lay stranded on its stone floor. Some were the size of small rowboats, others were three times as big, with triple sets of oars. I wondered who used them. Well, no one now, of course. The thin stream that flowed toward the center of the lake wasn't enough to float even the smallest of them.

Urbang led us to the back of the cave. I had my next surprise when I saw a rope dangling there. I lifted the lantern to see what it was connected to, but the rope continued up beyond the reach of my light, disappearing into the darkness. Urbang gave it a hearty tug, then said, "Now we wait for a bit. You might as well sit."

"What are we waiting for?" I asked.

She just smiled and said, "You'll see."

I rolled my eyes, but it wasn't nearly as effective as when Urbang did it. Lura and I sat. Urbang crouched, looking more froglike than usual.

After a few minutes I heard a sound from above. It was faint at first but grew steadily louder. In a little while, an enormous basket—as high as my waist and about five feet across—descended into the space next to the rope. It made me think of the baskets people use when they travel in hot-air balloons.

As the basket settled to the cave floor I could see that it was held by four ropes. These ropes met at a point about six feet above the basket, where they were woven together to form a single rope as thick as my arm. Dangling below the spot where the ropes met was a metal sphere.

"Climb in," said Urbang.

"Where are we going?" I asked.

Urbang smiled. "Up! Trust me, this way is easier than climbing!"

Once the three of us were settled in the basket, Urbang reached over and tugged on the rope again.

Instantly, we began to rise into the darkness.

INSIDE THE MOUNTAIN

At first the basket swayed and spun, but after we had gone up about twenty feet it stabilized. At the same time, the metal sphere that hung beneath the place where the four ropes merged began to glow, lighting the walls around us.

I gasped. We were in a circular shaft with a diameter barely larger than our basket. What had caused my gasp was the beautiful art that covered every square inch of the shaft. Most of it was paintings, but as we continued to rise we came to sections where the living stone had been carved so that the images appeared to emerge directly from the wall. I found myself turning in slow circles, eager not to miss anything.

Many of the images were water scenes—lovely valleys with wandering streams, or raging rivers, or sheltered ponds. Others were portraits. To my surprise these were divided about equally between Land People—all of them blue like

Lura—and Water People. Still others were of scenes that looked like real events, including one that showed a mix of about a dozen Land People and Water People sitting at a table together, clearly having a good time.

We came to a picture of a giant blue man holding a fountain from which gushed crystal water. Lura put her hand to her mouth and whispered, "That's Belaquian!"

When we had risen several feet above that image she shouted, "Stop!" But we had no control over the upward movement of the basket and so kept moving.

"What is it?" I asked.

Instead of answering me, she turned toward Urbang. "Why is there a picture of my mother on these walls?" she demanded.

I looked down, trying to see what Lura was referring to, but we had already risen above it.

"The art shows people, places, and events that have been important to us," said Urbang.

"Who did all this, anyway?" I asked. "And why do it in the dark?"

Urbang laughed. "It's not in the dark when someone is traveling through the shaft! Besides, why waste all this lovely space? It was perfect for decoration."

I wondered if the frog-woman really thought this amazing art was mere decoration, or if that was some aspect of the language thingy. But there was no time to talk about that, because we had reached the top of the shaft. I could see that the thick rope was being wound around a wooden pole held several feet above floor level by a pair of notched posts. Crank handles that extended from each side of the shaft were being turned by a pair of Water People. The last two or three feet of the shaft rose above the floor level. This part was constructed of stones mortared together, making it look like an old-fashioned well, if a particularly big one. We stopped rising when the edge of the basket was level with the top of this stone circle.

We had emerged into a large cavern. It was lit by dozens of small pots that held blue, smokeless flames. To my right a large opening showed a starry sky. Clearly we were now above the clouds that had obscured the crown of the cliffs when we looked at them from below.

We faced a crowd of at least a hundred Water People. The expressions on their faces varied. Some seemed surprised, some uneasy, others angry. At last one of them crossed to us. Clearly furious, he pointed at Lura and said, "Urbang Garglack, my desire to welcome you home is tainted like a soiled pond. How do you dare bring this girl into the Cavern of Waters?"

"I have come to speak to Belaquian," Lura replied.

A gasp ran through the crowd. Some of the women broke into tears.

"You dare?" croaked the Water Person who had approached us. "You dare, girl, to seek the Bringer of Waters after your blasphemies? We should throw you from the cliffs to crash with the dying River Sar into the mudbanks below!"

"Peace, Sir Kartanga," said Urbang, spreading her hands. "There are things you are not yet aware of."

"And there are things that have happened since you left that you have no idea of," replied Kartanga. This time I heard as much grief as anger in his voice. "And this girl must take part of the blame!"

"I never wanted to take Belaquian's place!" Lura cried. "I was put on the throne by Solarian and I have come to beg forgiveness."

"You must first look at what has happened!" Kartanga said bitterly. Turning to the cave dwellers, he shouted, "Step aside. Let her see!"

At his command the Water People clustered more closely together. In doing so they revealed a narrow stream that flowed to the opening in the cavern wall, then disappeared over the edge, creating the waterfall we had bathed in. Tracing the stream back in the other direction, I saw that it flowed from a spout carved into a stone basin about thirty feet in diameter.

From the center of the basin rose a tangle of what looked like tentacles made of solid stone. Winding around each other, the tentacles stretched up for about fifteen feet. On their tips rested a broad, circular platform, also made of stone. From the platform flowed a wavering stream that dropped with a feeble splash into the granite basin.

Even in that dim blue light, and from so far away, I could see holes torn through the platform, as if something had been wrenched from its surface.

"The fountain!" Lura cried. "It's here, just as my mother told me!" She dashed across the cavern to the basin, leaped over its edge, then splashed through the shallow water to the stone tentacles. Nimble as a gymnast, she climbed the web of stone that supported the platform. When she reached the top and scrambled onto the platform, her joy vanished. "It's gone!" she wailed.

Her words of despair echoed through the cavern.

I thought she should have realized this from the beginning, but I guess she had been overcome by hope. "He stole it, Hurricane! The fountain that gives us water has been stolen, just like your horn!"

The cave dwellers appeared stunned by her actions. A buzz of whispers rose from the group. Kartanga went to the edge of the basin and said, almost piteously, "You spoke the truth?"

"Of course I did!" she blazed. "Where is Belaquian? Has he been wounded? Weakened? Let me see him!"

Kartanga drew a long breath, exhaled, then said, "Belaquian is gone."

Urbang, who was next to me, groaned. Lura, still kneeling on top of that platform, leaned back as if she had been struck. Then she slowly climbed down the stone tentacles. I could see by the way she moved that something was broken deep inside her.

When she had rejoined us, I told Kartanga the story of how Aerobellan had been stolen, and how I had come to this world to look for it. Urbang picked up the tale from the time I had rescued her from the "sucky-sand." Lura remained mute, still wrapped in sorrow.

Kartanga shook his head. "We thought Belaquian had left in anger, deserting our world because it had deserted him in favor of this girl and her mother." He glanced toward the basin, the stone tentacles, the platform. "In our fear we misinterpreted the signs of struggle, the way the fountain-hold was damaged. We thought Belaquian had taken the fountain in anger. I should have known better. I see now that the master did not leave of his own free will. But who can abduct a god? The very question makes me tremble."

Kartanga turned to Lura. "You must understand how many times Belaquian conjured for us, in the scrying pool beneath the fountain, images of what took place in the valley. We saw your mother, then you, on the Throne of Waters. Many times I urged the Waterlord to blast you from the face of the world, but he would not, and I never understood why. Despite his mercy, you must face that it was for you and your mother that the people turned away, weakening Belaquian with every heart that abandoned him. That is why I felt such rage when I first saw you."

"I am more sorry for my part in all this than you can know," Lura said. "Can you understand that it was against my will?"

Kartanga placed his hands together and made a slight bow.

Something had been puzzling me, and I asked about it

now. "If Belaquian and the fountain are gone, why is there still water trickling from the fountainhold?"

"It comes from threads of magic that were left behind," said Kartanga. "But it is fading. Each day the flow diminishes."

"How many days has it been?" Urbang asked.

"Ten," replied Kartanga. "The ten most fearful days of my life." He looked out at the others and added, "Of all our lives."

"Is there anything else you can tell us about Belaquian's disappearance?" I asked.

"Only one thing, a very troubling thing that I do not understand. But I will show you if you wish to see it."

"Please," I said.

Kartanga led us past the fountainhold to a passage that extended into the depths of the cavern. In a little while I saw a glimmer of red reflecting on the walls ahead. A moment later we rounded a stone corner.

Pulsing ahead of us was a sphere of red light at least twice my height.

"This appeared the day Belaquian vanished," said Kartanga, his voice hushed.

"It's a Sphere of Passage," I whispered. "The thief *made* a Sphere of Passage!"

Kartanga turned to me. "I do not understand."

"Something like this is how I came here," I said. "The spheres lead from one world to another. From what

Zephron told me, it would take someone with immense power to create one of these."

Lura, who had followed close behind me, put a hand on my shoulder. I glanced at her. What kind of being were we facing? What were its powers?

And what were the chances of saving my mother now?

Though the pull of the horn made me long to keep moving immediately, we spent the rest of that day, and most of the next, in the cavern. This was because Lura and Urbang insisted they would be coming with me. This journey had changed a great deal since I had started out with Zephron. In the back of my mind I was constantly worrying about what had happened to him. Had the green sphere somehow rejected him, so that he was still in his cave, worrying about what was happening with me? And if he wasn't, what was going to happen if by some miracle I did manage to get the horn back? I sure wouldn't know how to blow the wind to life! And how about that time peg? We hadn't talked about it much. How long was it good for? Would its magic run out if I took too long getting back?

"Hurricane?" said Lura. "Are you all right?"

I had gotten so lost in my thoughts that her voice made me jump. "I'm fine," I muttered, not wanting to lay out all my worries. Despite my desire to push on, the fact that she and Urbang were coming with me was a relief. The problem was, it meant taking time to properly equip them for whatever we might find when we ventured through the red sphere. Preparation mainly consisted of providing heavy clothes to match my own cold-weather gear. As Zephron had taught me back when we packed in his cave, dealing with intense heat was easy, if possibly embarrassing—you just stripped down. But if the next world was freezing cold, we had to be ready for it.

Having accepted us, the cave dwellers proved generous, offering silks and furs that they stitched together to make protective garments. Kartanga himself gave us a lantern, saying, "This should last longer than the one you are carrying. After all, when you live inside a mountain, you learn a great deal about providing light."

I thanked him, not mentioning that the lantern I was carrying had come from another magical cave.

The Water People provided a small side cave for Lura and me to sleep in. As we were settling the first night, I said, "Lura, could you teach me how to do that Flow thing? I mean so we could create a Flow on our own? It might come in useful."

She thought for a moment. "It's an interesting idea. According to my mother, it's not something most people can manage. But since you've already been in the Flow with me, it might be possible. Let's try."

We worked on it for an hour. Unfortunately, nothing happened.

By the time we gave up we were exhausted. Which was just as well. Otherwise I doubt I would have slept at all.

By the middle of the next day we were ready to leave. The cave dwellers gathered to bid us farewell but did not follow as Kartanga led us to the scarlet sphere.

When we stood in front of the glowing globe, bracing ourselves to enter, I whispered to Lura, "I've done this once. It's weird, but it doesn't hurt. Honest."

What I thought but didn't say was *I wish we had a time peg for you, too.*

We thanked Kartanga for his help. In return, he placed his huge, flat hands together, bowed slightly, and said, "I wish you good fortune on your mission. For all our sakes."

I had told Lura and Urbang about how Zephron and I had been separated when I came through the first sphere. To try to avoid that, we had decided to join hands as we entered. Our hope was that if we held on to each other, we would make it through to the next world together.

I clasped Lura's slim blue fingers in my right hand. At the same time, Urbang wrapped her smooth webbed fingers around my left hand.

On a count of three, we walked forward into the sphere.

The passage was much like my first trip, save that this time I was flooded by red instead of green. The bigger difference was that when I came out on the other side, I was not alone. Urbang and Lura were still with me!

We emerged into darkness. Far worse than the darkness was the intense, bone-chilling cold. Not knowing what kind of world would greet us, we had not dressed for this. Now we tore open our packs and scrambled to get out our winter clothes. I had just pulled out my parka when Urbang cried, "Oh, children, this is far worse than I had imagined! I cannot . . . I cannot . . ."

Those were the last words she spoke before collapsing at our feet.

"I'D SUGGEST
THAT YOU SEEK DOONA"

"We have to get her out of here!" cried Lura. "No Water Person can abide such cold! She'll be dead in minutes!"

Desperately hoping we were moving fast enough, we managed to pull Urbang to her feet, then sling one of her arms over each of our shoulders. We dragged her back to the red sphere and stepped into it. An instant later we were in the Cavern of Waters.

Since Kartanga had already returned to the main space, no one was there to greet us.

"Stay with Urbang," I told Lura, who was already rubbing the frog-woman's hands. "I'll get help." I raced back to the main portion of the cave, shouting, "Kartanga! Kartanga, Urbang is in trouble!"

Kartanga came running, followed by several other Water People.

"It was too cold on the other side of the sphere," I gasped. "Urbang collapsed and she's—"

They didn't wait for me to finish, simply rushed past. By the time I caught up with them, a pair of Water People were huddled against Urbang, pressing their bodies close to warm her up. To my relief, her eyes were open and she was trying to talk.

"Hush, friend," said Kartanga. "Wait a bit."

The two Water People got Urbang to her feet and began to walk her in circles.

Kartanga came to stand next to me. "She will be all right after a time. We just need to get her blood moving again. Thank you for getting her back here so quickly. The cold must have been truly bitter where you went."

"It was horrible," Lura said.

"Then you cannot go on?" Kartanga asked.

Lura shook her head. "It will be hard, but Hurricane and I can manage it. But I don't think any Water Folk can survive there."

Kartanga frowned. "I hate to think of you going ahead on your own."

"We have no choice," I said.

Urbang, still supported by the two others, staggered over to us. "I am so sorry," she said. "Our people are simply not meant to deal with cold that fierce. Thank you for getting me back here."

"We will miss you," I said, "but we have to move on. And we should do it quickly."

I didn't mention it, but I was already nervous that someone might find the backpacks we had left behind and steal them. Or maybe a wind would come up and blow away my jacket, which I had dropped when Urbang collapsed.

"I understand," said Urbang.

An odd thought came to me. I hesitated, then said, "Do Water People hug?"

"Of course," said Urbang.

"Then may I hug you good-bye?"

She drew me to her. I thought with amazement of how quickly I had come to trust and rely on someone who was so very, very different from me.

With a hint of a smile, Urbang turned to Lura and said, "How about goddesses? Do they hug farewell?"

"Oh, hush," said Lura.

Then she gave Urbang a big hug.

And then we did the only thing we could do.

We went back through the sphere.

My first action on the other side was to dig out my lantern and say, "Light!" We needed its glow to help us struggle into our cold-weather clothes. That struggle was horribly uncomfortable, because the clothes had grown frigid in the time it took us to return Urbang to the Cavern of Waters.

Even when I had the clothes on I was trembling. I think it was partly from the cold but also from what had happened to Urbang. I had lost Zephron and had been grateful that Urbang was going to join us. Now it was just me and Lura, a couple of kids out to save two worlds that were in danger. I pushed the thought aside. I needed to clear my mind so I could catch the trail of the horn. If I couldn't find that, we were truly lost.

It didn't take long. "It went that way," I said, pointing to our left.

"I know," said Lura.

"You know?" I asked in surprise.

"Something happened to me in Belaquian's cavern, Hurricane. It was as if something woke up inside me. I didn't want to say anything about it until I was sure, but now that we're in this new place, I am certain. I can sense the fountain in the same way that you sense the horn."

I was startled but quickly realized this was a good thing. "If it pulls you the same way the horn pulls me, that will help us keep going," I said.

"I agree," replied Lura. With that, we trudged off in the direction we had agreed on. In a few minutes a wind, bitterly cold, began to buffet us. I could tell it did not come from Aerobellan; it did not speak to my heart.

After a while, Lura said, "Maybe we should only use one lantern at a time. We don't know how long we'll be traveling."

"Good idea," I replied.

She turned hers off, then handed it to me. "Put it in my pack," she said. I understood at once: my doing it would be faster than her having to take off her pack to do it herself.

And that mattered, because neither of us wanted to stay in this stinging cold a second longer than necessary.

The darkness felt thick and heavy. We pressed together for the tiny bit of additional heat we could offer each other. Long grass, blasted and frozen, snapped under our feet like uncooked spaghetti. The ground beneath that brittle grass was hard as granite.

Though we had left Lura's world in the morning, we had entered this world at night. At least, I assumed it was night. But we couldn't treat it as night because we were wide-awake.

I hoped it would get light soon.

It didn't.

We forged on. What else was there to do? If not for the pull of the horn, I might have given up. I was glad Lura could now sense the trail, too; it boosted my confidence.

We did stop once, when we came to a huge boulder that could protect us from the wind. Huddled in its shelter, we had a small meal. The food was so cold we had to melt it in our mouths before we could chew it.

"I think your lantern is getting dimmer," Lura said.

I studied it for a minute, then said, "You're right. But it shouldn't be. Zephron told me it would last for days!" Feeling uneasy, I said, "Let's check the one Kartanga gave us."

Lura pulled it from her pack and pressed her thumb on the top. Like the lantern I carried, it was dimmer than it had been before.

"Different world, different rules?" suggested Lura.

"I don't like it" was all I could say.

"If they're both going to get dimmer at the same rate, we might as well use this one while we can," she said.

With both lanterns out, we resumed our journey. As we trudged on, I found myself wishing we had a way to keep track of time, which made me wonder if time worked the same way in this world that it did in my world, or Lura's. Did the time peg keep track of all that stuff?

After a while we came to some frozen water. In the dim glow of our lanterns it was impossible to tell whether it was a small pond or a vast lake.

I spotted a small shack at the edge of the water and said, "Well, there must be people of some sort in this world."

"Small ones, based on the look of that place," Lura replied.

"Maybe, maybe not. I'm guessing this is some kind of play fort that kids made. I doubt anyone lives here."

"So you think it's safe to go in?"

"Probably. But we should knock first, just in case."

We knocked and shouted but got no answer. The hope of getting some shelter from the cold was too much to resist, so we pushed open the door, which was no higher than my shoulder. The shack held no furniture, not even a bed or a chair. And the ceiling was so low we couldn't stand up straight. But it was well sealed against the wind, which was all we really wanted just then. It felt strange to me to want to get *away* from the wind.

We slumped to the floor and dug out our blankets; mine

from Zephron's cave, Lura's a gift from the Water People. Without discussing it, we spooned together and wrapped both blankets as snugly around ourselves as we could.

"I'm not sure I can sleep," whispered Lura.

"I'm not sure we'll wake up if we do," I replied. "But we have to get some rest."

"All right. But if we do manage to sleep, whoever wakes up first has to rouse the other."

"Agreed," I said.

Not long after that, I was asleep.

As I said, exhaustion has its uses.

I was woken by Lura shaking my shoulder. "Hurricane," she said softly. "Hurricane!"

"I'm awake," I muttered, shivering.

"It's still dark. Shouldn't it be light by now?"

My first thought was that she was right: it should be. But then I thought a bit more. "Maybe not. In the far north of my world, night lasts for a couple of months when it's winter. Given how cold it is, I figure we must be in the far north of this world."

I was wrong about that, as we would discover later that frigid "day."

We walked for hours. At least, it felt that way. On the

plus side, the wind had died down and the land was fairly friendly—low hills and no serious obstacles. On the minus side, the lanterns continued to grow dimmer. Still, they were bright enough to let us know when we came to a narrow road. This one was paved, not like the dirt roads of Lura's world.

"If we follow this it will probably lead to a town," I said.

"Would that be a good thing?" asked Lura.

"Hard to say. With luck, we might find shelter from the cold. Or we might get captured, like I was in your world."

Lura made a face, then said, "I suppose it doesn't make any difference if it's a good idea or not. We have to follow the trail, wherever it leads."

As it turned out, the pull of the horn and the fountain led us only a short distance along the road before it veered off into a wooded area. I noticed that the trees still had most of their leaves, which would have seemed unlikely if it was actually winter. The thought was worrisome.

After crossing two or three frozen streams, we came out of the woods. Soon after that we reached a wooden fence. We stepped over it easily—it was barely knee-high. A bit farther on we spotted a soft glow. Drawing closer, we saw that it came from windows in a house.

"What do you think?" I asked.

"Do you mean, should we go and ask for shelter?" Lura answered.

"Yep."

Teeth chattering, she said, "Definitely."

We headed for the windows, which meant leaving the trail. I let out a cry at the physical pain this caused me.

"I know," whispered Lura. "I feel that now, too."

As we drew close to the house, which I was starting to think was oddly small, we came to a metal contraption.

"What's that?" asked Lura.

I moved my lantern so I could get a better view, then said, "Looks like a very small, very old-fashioned tractor."

"A what? I mean, I heard you. But that word doesn't mean anything."

Whatever powers of understanding a person picked up by coming through the spheres clearly had limits. But how do you explain a tractor to someone who's never seen one?

"It's a machine," I started.

"A what?"

I sighed and tried again. "It's, um . . . a kind of tool. It sort of works by itself. Well, not completely. . . . This needs fuel and someone to steer it." Thinking back to when I lived in Mississippi, I added, "It can be used to haul carts and plow fields."

"Oh, stop. If you don't want to tell me what it is, don't. But it's too cold for stupid jokes."

"All right, never mind," I said, feeling grouchy. "But I can tell you this much: if that's what I think it is, then the people here are way smaller than us."

"Well, I had already guessed that from the hut," said

Lura. "Maybe we shouldn't go up to the house. We'll probably scare whoever is inside."

"I still think we should try."

"People are dangerous when they're afraid, Hurricane."

"Well, I'm pretty much terrified all the time now, so I should be really dangerous! Come on, let's give it a try."

As we drew closer we could see that the house really was small. Not small like my mom's little place in Mississippi had been. Small as in bigger than a dollhouse but not big enough to qualify even as a cozy cottage. The roof was only a few feet above my head! Though the front door was a bit bigger than the door of that shack where we had slept, it still came only about to my chin.

I squatted to knock.

No answer.

I knocked again.

No answer.

"We should go," said Lura.

"The lights are on, there should be someone home," I said stubbornly. I tried one more time and was rewarded by a scuffling sound from inside. Then someone called, "Who's there?"

Trying to think of what Zephron would have said, I answered, "Travelers, seeking shelter."

"Travelers from where?"

How to answer? Say we came from another world? Whoever was inside would think I was crazy. On the other hand, anyone who opened the door would immediately know we weren't from around these parts!

While I was trying to figure out what to say, Lura squatted beside me and called, "We come from a distant land and need shelter from the wind and cold."

"Then I'd suggest that you seek Doona!"

"Who's Doona?" I asked, shouting to be heard above a sudden gust of wind.

But that was the end of the conversation. Lura and I both knocked several times but could get nothing more from the person inside the house. I felt an urge to kick in the door but restrained myself and merely yelled a very bad word before we turned back toward the path.

As we passed the tractor again I had an idea. Handing my lantern to Lura, I said, "Hold this for a second."

"Why?"

"Just hold it, will you? I want to check something out."

She took my lantern and I climbed onto the tractor. Doing so didn't bring me much higher off the ground, but I thought it might be enough to give me a wider view. "Okay, hand me the lantern."

She did as I asked and I held it up. "Hah!" I said in triumph.

"What did you see?" she asked as I climbed down.

"There's a barn over there. I figured there might be. Tractors and barns kind of go together. Maybe we can shelter in there."

Fighting the wind, we stumbled our way to the barn. It

was larger than the house, as barns tend to be. The wide doors at the front were held shut by a simple hasp with a wooden peg through its metal loop. I removed the peg and pulled the door open.

From the pitch-dark interior, an angry voice shouted, "Who's there? Answer quickly or suffer the consequences!"

AMBERJON

I was too tired and cold to worry about consequences. Still holding the lantern, I stepped into the barn and said, "We are just trying to get out of the storm."

"Great Galloping Gazoompas!" cried the voice. "As if the cold and the dark weren't enough, are there now giants in the land?"

"We are only passing through," said Lura. "We mean you no harm."

"I've heard that before. And I've said it often enough myself. Not that it usually did me any good. Still, since I can see you, I might as well let you see me. I'll trust you to use your great size to protect me should the householder decide to venture out and take care of his stock. It would be unseemly of you to simply crush me."

A moment later a dim glow, not much brighter than what came from our ever-weakening lanterns, blossomed a few feet away from us. Sitting on a bed of purple straw and holding a lantern of his own was a youngish-looking man not more than three feet tall. He was dressed in ragged robes. Scraps of cloth were bound around his feet in place of shoes, and gloves without fingers protected the palms of his hands. Sharp, steady eyes peered out from a lemon-yellow face that seemed to have more nose than it needed. Vivid scarlet hair, parted in the middle, hung down to his shoulders.

In the low light, I could make out a green animal in a stall behind him. Setting aside its color, it was a bit like a cow . . . if a cow was a third of its regular size and had a head shaped like a bowling ball. In that way, it reminded me of the "horses" in Lura's world—close enough to consider it a cow, but just barely.

"Have a seat," said the little man, gesturing toward another stack of straw. Or maybe it was hay. Since it was purple and the light was so low, it was hard for me to tell, despite my country-boy roots.

The little man stood and said, "My name is Amberjon."

"I'm Hurricane."

"And I'm Lura."

"Pleased to meet you both."

"You don't seem to have a problem with us being, um . . . giants," said Lura.

Amberjon shrugged. "I've spent most of my life in the circus. I'm used to freaks."

I felt like I should be offended but decided it wasn't worth getting upset over.

"So what brings you huge, lumbering creatures to our dark and benighted world?" he asked.

"You seem to be taking the darkness lightly," I replied, stupidly proud of myself for answering his pun with one of my own.

"I mentioned the circus, right? My first job was as a clown. I have to take things lightly."

"What's a circus?" Lura asked.

Clearly the world we were in now was more like mine than it was like hers.

"It's a kind of show," I told her. "Clowns are supposed to make you laugh."

"Or terrify you," put in Amberjon. "I often did that, especially with the little ones. It was fun but I always felt a bit guilty afterward."

"If you belong with a circus, why are you sitting here in a barn?" I asked.

"It's a long story. And please note that I asked you first. So why don't you sit down and tell me? It's also a long night. . . . In fact, it appears it may last forever. So we have at least until we freeze to death. Or starve. Whichever comes first."

The little man's casual attitude seemed strange. But telling our story, and getting his in return, seemed the most sensible thing to do.

"We have some food," said Lura. "If you're hungry."

I could have clobbered her for that, since our supplies weren't that plentiful. But then I remembered Mom's insistence on sharing food . . . and also remembered her teaching me that doing so was one of the best ways to make friends with someone.

"I'm hungry enough," said Amberjon. "But I'm guessing your food is fairly hard. On account of freezing. I can build a fire. Wouldn't normally do that in a barn, for fear of burning the place down, which is not good manners and would not be fair to our host. But since the best I can manage now is about a quarter of what a fire should be—or maybe an eighth, by this time—I think we're safe enough."

He gathered a pile of the purple stuff, then reached behind him. That was when I realized he also had a backpack, which made sense as he had obviously been traveling. He pulled a pair of metal rods from the pack, held them over the straw, then struck them together. A brief burst of flame shot into the straw, which began to smolder. He blew on the straw. It caught fire, but the green flames were slow and weak.

"Frizzled flakbarts," Amberjon muttered. "Even worse than last time. Well, it'll have to do. Drag out your provisions and let's see if we can warm them up a bit."

We did as he asked, and in not too much time we were slowly warming—or, more accurately, *thawing*—some fruit and meat over the wobbly green flames.

"Now, while we cook—and I use the term loosely—this fine food, I think it would be a good time for you to tell me your story. After all, I did ask first. You talk, we eat, then

I talk in turn. It will be jolly good fun, or if not, at least something to do while we wait for the end of the world."

With that invitation, our tale came tumbling out, complete with interruptions, contradictions, and corrections. When we had finished, Amberjon shook his head. "Wind gone; water, too. Even worse than I had thought. I would say you were on a fool's errand, seeking this horn and this fountain, but since I, too, am seeking something, who am I to talk? However, I will, I promise. Talk, I mean. As soon as we down some of these welcome provisions. I won't eat much. Given my size compared to you, how could I?"

We huddled close to the pathetic fire and ate. A couple of times I tried to get Amberjon to start on his own story, but both times he said, "Food is food, talk is talk. I prefer not to mix the two."

This seemed strange to me, since for all my life meals had been a time to talk, maybe the best time. But we were hardly in a position to argue with him.

When the last bit had been eaten, Amberjon carefully sucked his fingers clean—counting his thumb, he had only four on each hand—then said, "All right, now it's my turn. To start with, I was born thousands of kleektaks from here."

What I actually heard was a combination of "kleek-taks" and "miles." It was confusing but clearly my brain was starting to understand how words were being translated for it.

Ignoring my confusion, Amberjon continued his story.

Mom had seven kids in all. I was the last . . . which meant I was just one more mouth to feed. So, as was not unusual in our village, I was sold to a passing group. To my good fortune, it was a circus. I shudder to think what my life would have been like had I been sold to a group of gravediggers!

For a long time I did all sorts of jobs. I take some pride in the fact that I was the youngest clown ever at the Circus Flamboyicus!

Despite that, I also had to help put up the tents. Alas, working with a sledgehammer was never my strong point and after a number of injuries to myself and others, I was excused from that task. Eventually I was apprenticed to Gramps Branzancus, our story master and fortune-teller. His command of old tales was amazing—he could hold an audience silent for hours. As a fortune-teller, he was mostly a fraud. But only mostly. He taught me the difference between what he did that was real and what was for show. Most of all he taught me to always give the customer hope, even if he or she is heading for a flaming catastrophe. Or, as it has turned out in the case of our world now, an un-flaming catastrophe.

We worked together for years, and I loved him like a father. More than my real father, actually, since Dad was the one who sold me, while Gramps Branzancus was the one who taught me. And which matters more in the end, eh?

I learned minor magics and major deceptions and came to relish both.

The only thing Gramps and I really disagreed on was Doona. Most people of Gramps's generation believed Doona was the keeper of the Great Hearth of the World, the source of all heat and light. I thought this was a bunch of hooey, in line with the tricks and scams and minor magics we performed on our customers. These days belief in Doona has so waned that her name has become a symbol of futility. If you want help with a problem that is beyond help, people say, "I'd suggest that you seek Doona."

This was my own belief. Then one night Gramps brought me to his wagon and with a serious face said, "Amberjon, I will not be with you much longer."

"Don't say that!" I cried.

"Don't be foolish," he replied sharply. "Life is what it is. So is death. Soon I will be gone. You are the son I never had, so it falls to you to take on the burden I have carried all my life."

"Burden?" I asked, truly puzzled now.

He slid from his arm a silver band that he had worn for as long as I had known him. Unlike other ornaments, rings and necklaces and so on, this one he had never taken off.

Holding it between us, he said, "In my younger years I was an apprentice of Doona, one of nine. Do not scoff! Doona is real and worthy of your devotion. This armband came from her. She herself slid it onto my arm in preparation for a time that is yet to come. We may play many tricks on our customers, but you well know that the future is not entirely hidden from us. I tell you as sure as I am sitting here that a dark time approaches. When that day arrives, the Nine will be called. I used to hope it would not come in my lifetime. Now I regret that it did not, for I had rather the burden fall to me than to you. But I will be gone. So it is to you that I must pass this task."

I was silent for a time.

"Will you accept it?" he asked at last.

"Of course," I replied, not thinking about what the consequences might be.

"Extend your arm."

I did as he asked. As he slid the band up my arm I felt a strange tingle that could only be magic. Gramps leaned close and whispered, "When the time comes, you will know."

He was with me for a while longer, which was a blessing. When he left me, which was a grief, I continued with the circus.

And then the darkness came.

It was not long ago, as days are counted. One morning the sun was late to rise, and dim when it did. On that morning-that-wasn't-a-morning, this armband blazed with a heat that woke me screaming from my sleep. I knew then that the darkness was coming. And so it has. Light has grown weak. Fires have faded. A terrible coldness grips our world. In the days since this began I have followed the path on which the armband leads me. When I deviate, it burns. As long as I move in the right direction, it does not hurt.

So your stories make sense to me. Though "I'd suggest that you seek Doona" has become a term of mockery, doing exactly that is now our only hope.

I am but a half-real, half-fraudulent minor magician and fortune-teller. But the journey I am on was handed to me by the one person in the world whom I truly loved and honored, and I cannot turn my back on it. I have little doubt that our paths lie in the same direction. Therefore, I believe we should travel through this darkness together.

Lura and I looked at each other. She nodded. I nodded back. And that was how we became a group of three.

17

SPIRIT OF FLAME

The trail now carried us into rough terrain, a mountainous area where we seemed to be walking endlessly upward. Because of the darkness, we could tell almost nothing of the countryside beyond the glow of our lanterns. The only thing we knew for sure was that it was strewn with boulders. The trees, on the other hand, grew smaller and fewer as we climbed, eventually vanishing altogether as we passed the timberline.

I had feared that Amberjon, with his short legs, might slow us down. To my surprise he kept up without complaint; sometimes he even got ahead of us.

With day and night indistinguishable, we had no way to tell how long we traveled. We slept twice after leaving the barn, which seemed to indicate two "nights." But the path was so rugged, the cold so fierce, it might have been only that we had grown overly tired, and but a single day had passed.

Amberjon started a fire whenever we stopped to rest. Each time the flames were weaker than the time before.

The first night, he tried to do a few tricks for us, simple ones that I knew from home—pulling a coin from behind Lura's ear, that kind of thing.

They failed.

"Sorry," he said. "My fingers are so cold I can't move them the way the trick demands." He grabbed his feet, as if to warm his toes and fingers at the same time, and grew silent. After a moment he said, almost shyly, "Have you ever done a meld?"

"What's a meld?" I asked.

"It's a way to link minds . . . light to light, my internal flame to yours."

"It sounds like entering the Flow," said Lura.

This led to some confusion, but after a bit of back-and-forth, we realized they were talking about the same thing.

"I didn't want to suggest it right away," said Amberjon. "But now that we've been together for a time I feel comfortable with you. So I think it would be a good idea if we try one. How good are you at it? Can you do a walking meld?"

"A what?" Lura and I asked together.

"A walking meld is one where you don't have to be in physical contact to maintain the meld. It would come in handy if we get separated in this darkness."

The idea disturbed me, since I still wasn't entirely comfortable with linking minds. But I could definitely see why it could be useful. "We should try it," I said.

Two somewhat disturbing hours later—disturbing for me, at least—we had it. It was exciting to be able to speak to Lura and Amberjon by thought only.

Now walk away, said Amberjon, his words forming in our minds. *Go in opposite directions.*

Why? thought Lura.

To test the connection.

We did as he suggested. I felt our link grow weaker and started to panic, afraid of getting lost in the dark. Sensing my fear, Amberjon thought, *Okay, move back to me.*

When Lura and I returned to our pathetic campfire he ended the connection.

"That was good for a first time for the three of us," he said. "And as we practice we'll be able to keep the link over greater distances. But it gets tiring, doesn't it?"

"Definitely," I said. "But how come you knew how to do that to begin with?"

"Am I not a clown who was trained by Gramps Branzancus?" replied Amberjon with a chuckle.

The only thing that gave us hope as we struggled against the wind and the cold was the certainty all three of us felt that we were getting close to our goal. Because of the walking meld, which we practiced a couple more times, it was a certainty that we shared at the deepest level.

This burning in the blood kept us going, let us walk on when walking seemed impossible, even find the courage to push each other forward. We lifted one foot at a time in an endless rhythmic pattern, without thought but with incredible effort.

Then our lanterns went out, just totally died. The darkness was now complete and utter. It would have been so easy to stop then, to just lie down and let the cold take us.

"Don't move until we form a meld," said Amberjon.

We gathered close to get it started. Once we were linked, I thought to the others, *We should get to our hands and knees and crawl, so we don't fall over some unexpected cliff.*

On hands and knees is how we came at last to Doona's cave. We didn't realize, at first, that it was a cave, only that we were out of the wind. It could simply have been a large rock shielding us. Except I felt something different, something inside myself.

The horn has been here, I thought to the others.

Yes, yes, I feel that way about the fountain, replied Lura.

It was Amberjon who seemed most affected. Speaking

out loud, he said, "This is the place! Oh, I should have believed Gramps. I should have believed him!"

Still on hands and knees, we inched forward. Though it was not warm, just being out of the wind was an enormous relief. We felt a rock wall to our right and kept our shoulders against that, using it as a guide. Then, as we came around a curve, I caught my breath at the sight of a glimmer of light ahead of us! After Zephron's cave, and the Cavern of Waters, light in a cave was not that much of an astonishment. It was finding any light at all in this dark, dark world that made me gasp.

Though the glow was hardly enough to let us see where we were going, we picked up speed, eager to get closer. After several yards we turned a sharp corner.

We had entered a large chamber. At the back of the chamber rose an altar carved from the living rock. Scattered across its surface were bits of wood that danced with a strange golden flame.

In front of the altar, in a stone chair, sat a very old woman. She was closer to my size than to Amberjon's. Her long hair was gray and stringy, her face so gaunt that her high cheekbones and hawklike nose stood out in bold relief. She wore an ill-fitting yellow robe that hung loosely on her bony shoulders. Even here, out of the wind, the air was achingly cold and I wondered how she had kept from freezing in only that robe.

Slowly, she turned her head in our direction. Her dark

eyes glittered, but her face showed a pain so profound I wanted to look away. I found I could not. Amberjon, Lura, and I got to our feet and went forward. When we were directly in front of the woman, Amberjon bowed and said in a soft voice, "Doona?"

The old woman raised her eyebrows. Her own voice little more than a croak, she said, "I think I used to be called that, back before things were so dark and cold. But how can I remember anything when it's so cold?"

"Why don't you warm your hands over the fire?" Lura asked, indicating the glowing wood on the stone altar.

A look of surprise crossed the woman's face, as if she had not realized the flames were there. "Yes," she murmured, "that would be good!" But when she tried to rise, she could not move. It was as if she was tied to the chair. "I forgot," she whispered. "I can't. It's too bad, isn't it?"

"Yes," I said softly. "It is. But why can't you get up?"

"I don't remember. I used to be able to." The tiniest of smiles tugged at her mouth. "I was happier then. The fire was bigger and the cave was warm." Her voice broke. "Now it's so cold . . . so *horribly* cold!"

Amberjon stepped closer. Moving slowly, he placed a hand on her arm. Instantly he cried out in pain and leaped back. "She is held by strong magic," he said. "Magic so far beyond the kind I know, it makes my head spin."

We stood in silence until Lura turned to Amberjon and said, "Your armband."

"What about it?"

"Give it to her. See if anything happens."

I was impressed. Even if it didn't work, it was a good idea.

Amberjon undid the various buttons and cords that held his multiple robes closed against the cold. Shivering, he pulled them away. I was surprised to see how muscular he was. The armband gleamed dully on his right bicep. He slid it down, rearranged his robes, then went to Doona and dropped the silver band into her hand.

Her eyes grew wide. Sweat began to form on her brow—an odd thing, given how cold the cave was. She shook her head, first slowly, then almost as violently as a dog shakes when it comes out of the water.

"Who are you?" she asked, looking at Amberjon.

"Amberjon Elderworth. My teacher was Jartenmir Branzancus. The armband I just placed in your hand came to me from him."

The old woman closed her eyes and her face passed through a series of contortions. Then, with a gasp, she cried, "And I am Doona!"

She shook her head again, as if trying to throw something off. "That's right!" she repeated, with a note of triumph. "I am Doona Warmheart, Keeper of the Flame! Good stranger, you have unlocked my mind. Can you unlock my body as well?"

Amberjon knelt and touched his forehead to the hem of her robe. "Though I am yours to command, alas, such magic is not within my grasp."

She sighed and nodded, then said, "I remember Jartenmir well. He has left us, I presume?"

"Yes, about a year ago. I loved him very much."

"As did I. As I loved all who have worn the nine bands. My heart rejoices that you have reached me, Amberjon. Yet I am filled with dread at what has happened."

"What *has* happened?" I asked. "Can you remember now?"

Doona closed her eyes. The loss and regret that twisted her face made me feel guilty for asking. But we had to know.

"A man came to my cave. He said his name was Mokurra. He spoke to me of worlds beyond worlds, then sang a song of sorrow. But the song was a spell and once I was bound by it, Mokurra seized Spirit of Flame, the torch that is the source of our world's warmth and light, from the wall above the altar." She hung her head. "I am scorched with shame by my failure."

After a moment she opened her eyes. Looking past Amberjon at Lura and me, she said, "I suppose the people advised you to seek me out. That's what they would say to anyone on a hopeless quest."

"Yes, they did," Lura replied gently.

Doona sighed. "They loved me once, long ago. Now I am simply a tale told to children, a jest to tease the foolish. I am weak from their indifference and thus had too little strength when the challenge came."

She struggled to rise. But though Amberjon had broken some of the spell that held her, she still could not leave the chair. Finally she fell back and said, "But what is your story? What has brought you to my forgotten and forsaken cave?"

Once again, Lura and I poured out our stories. When we finished, Doona sighed, then said, "Worlds grow and the old gods fade, or move on to another, newer world that needs them. When they do, they are replaced by protectors. I am one such, and it sounds as if your Zephron was also, Hurricane. I think this is as it must be. People have to move forward to take charge of their own destinies. Still, the old days had a sweetness to them. Back then the people would come to me with their problems and usually I could help. But eventually they became too wise and felt they no longer needed me. So I stayed in my cave and guarded Spirit of Flame. Now it is gone and the world I came to serve is dying."

Doona closed her eyes. "I was once a being of power. Now, alas, I can do little to help you. Instead, I ask a pledge. When you find the horn you seek, and the fountain you speak of, I am certain Spirit of Flame will be with them. Bring it back, please. This world that I came to serve will not last much longer without it."

"We'll do our best," I said. Notice I did not say, "I guarantee it." You can't guarantee you'll succeed. All you can guarantee is that you'll try as hard as you can.

Doona gave me a wan smile and said, "Thank you."

"Is there anything else you can tell us?" Lura asked.

"Only this: Once the thief had the torch, he went behind the altar, then far into the cave, where he worked some great magic. I could not see what he did, but the very air was hot with it. The floor of the cave shook and I sensed a change in the fabric of the world, something I had not felt in all the years since I first came here."

"Then that is the path we must follow," Amberjon said.

"Extend your arm, please," said Doona.

Amberjon did as the woman requested. She slipped the silver band over his hand, then slid it up his arm and said, "Now go with all my blessings, and all my hopes."

"Thank you, dear lady," murmured Amberjon. Then he stepped away.

Next Doona gestured to Lura and me and said, "You other two, you so young for the task, please approach. Kneel, if you would."

We did as she asked. Reaching forward, she placed a hand on each of our heads. I felt a jolt of power and a surge of warmth.

"May the elder powers go with you," she murmured. Then she lifted her hands and said, "Now go! Worlds are dying, and you have no time to dally. Behind the altar you'll find the way to the next world."

Lura and I stood and joined Amberjon. Together, we walked around the altar and farther into the cave, which continued for a great distance. It was easy to see the way because a rich blue light filled the space. We rounded a curve and there it was: a Sphere of Passage.

What we did not see until we were closer was the message carved into the floor in front of it:

MADE IT THIS FAR? I'M IMPRESSED. LET'S SEE HOW YOU DO IN PETRONIA!

Who was this thief, this Mokurra? Was he mocking us . . . or trying to lure us on? What kind of game was he playing?

I shook my head, then turned to Lura and Amberjon. "Shall we?"

The magician's face was grim. "What choice do we have?"

"Where the fountain has gone, I go," said Lura.

I held out my hands.

Lura and Amberjon took them.

Hoping no one would be left behind, we walked into the swirling blue.

18

PETRONIA

We stepped out into . . . nothing. Wherever the blue sphere had delivered us, it was not a world, at least not in any sense of that word that I understood. A dimly lit mist surrounded us, and not just from head to foot. It was under our feet, too. Which is to say, we were standing on nothing.

"What is this place?" Lura whispered.

"No idea," I replied. "But I don't like it."

"I don't, either," said Amberjon. "What I like even less is the idea of drifting apart from each other and getting separated in this zebbergidden mess. You two wouldn't happen to have a rope with you, by any chance? Might be a good idea to link ourselves."

"I have one in my pack," I said, working to keep my voice level. Had the blue sphere been another trap? Had we fallen into a place that was not really a *place*, just some bizarre limbo? Was this what had happened to Zephron?

"The rope?" said Amberjon.

"We're starting to float apart," Lura added, sounding alarmed.

Realizing that I had been drifting in my mind just as my body was drifting in this gray space, I pulled my pack from my back. I was tempted to let go of it, figuring it would float. But could I really count on that? I had no idea what the rules were here. What if I let go and rather than floating, my pack plummeted out of sight? Deciding not to chance it, I held the pack tight with one hand while I fished out the rope with the other. Holding one end, I tossed the remaining coil to Amberjon, who was closest to me. He caught it easily, gripped the part that extended toward me, and tossed the rest toward Lura. She was floating somewhere beyond him and when she reached for it she missed.

"That's all right," said Amberjon calmly. "We'll do it again."

While I worked on knotting my end of the rope around my waist, Amberjon rewound the rest and once more tossed it to Lura.

It didn't reach. She had drifted too far.

"Hurricane!" she cried.

"We'll get you!" I shouted, violating my own rule about not promising something I wasn't sure I could deliver. But Lura needed support more than truth in that moment. Then I remembered using the rope in Lura's world to save Urbang.

"Amberjon," I said, "I don't know how much magic you really have, but I do know the rope can stretch as needed."

At the same time, I tried to haul myself toward Lura by pulling on the rope that connected me to Amberjon. Major mistake! Doing that took *me* closer to Amberjon, but at the same time pulled *him* away from Lura!

"Hurricane!" Lura cried again.

Letting go of the rope, I began to stroke against the mist as if I was trying to swim. The stuff separated into slender gray tendrils that swirled around my hands and feet. It was like one of those dreams where you run and run but can't move forward. Except I *was* moving . . . just with excruciating slowness.

"I see what you're doing," Lura said, and started to imitate my swimming motions. For a long time it seemed as if we were at a standstill. We had no way to measure our movement, no way to mark progress, nothing that would let me say, "Ah, good, she passed that tree. Things are getting better." We just paddled against the mist. We were getting closer together but our movement could be measured in inches. Fractions of inches.

"Biskoffski!" cried Amberjon. "Got it!"

He hurled the rope again and this time the end went straight to Lura's hand. She cried out in relief as she grabbed it. All three of us began to haul on the rope, which brought us together in less than a minute. With Amberjon squished between Lura and me, we had what might have been the strangest group hug in history.

When we released the hug—but not each other's hands—Amberjon said, "Can you feel it?"

I knew at once what he meant. Now that my heart had stopped pounding I could definitely sense the pull of the horn. "Yes!" I said.

"I can, too," said Lura. "Clearly the thief came this way. But what is this place?"

"Place, Not Place, it makes no difference," said Amberjon. "We know the way to go."

"Yes, but let's get ourselves securely tied together first," said Lura. "I don't ever want to go through *that* again!"

Once we were safely linked by the rope, we started out, using my painfully slow swimming movement to go forward. It was impossible to mark time, or distance, or even direction. We might have gone in circles had it not been for the compelling pull of the stolen objects.

We felt no thirst, perhaps because the mist created a permanent sensation of being slightly damp. And we were always warm, which was a pleasant change. But we feared hunger was coming, as there would be no way to replenish our food supply once it was gone.

When we slept it was two at a time, the third always staying awake. We worried that if we drifted too far from the path the stolen objects had taken, we might lose the feel of their pull. This way, if we started to drift, whoever kept watch could wake the others.

After the fourth time we slept I noticed that Lura was strangely quiet.

"You all right?" I asked, realizing it was a stupid question even as the words left my mouth.

She shook her head. "I had a dream."

"About being stuck here?"

"No. I dreamed I saw Belaquian. His eyes were closed, and pain had pulled down the corners of his mouth. I feared he was dead, but then I heard his voice. It thundered in my ears and filled me with joyous fear. 'Lura,' he said, 'I need your help.'

"'How can I help?' I cried. 'You are a god, and I have destroyed you.'

"In my dream I rose from my sleep and sailed through darkness until I came to him. I was afraid but could not help myself. I reached out to touch him. When I did, the dream ended. My mind went blank and I felt loss like a knife in my heart."

Gray tendrils of mist curled around her as she huddled into herself. I wanted to reach out to her, but when she turned to face me I saw a fire in her eyes that had never been there before. She was different, and it frightened me. "I feel him calling," she said.

"Then we had better keep going," replied Amberjon, who had been floating silently nearby.

It was shortly after the fifth sleep that I heard a voice say, "Look! There's people!"

At first I thought it was my imagination. Then I saw

Lura's and Amberjon's faces and knew they had heard it, too.

We moved closer together.

"What's going on?" whispered Lura.

"I don't know, but I don't like it," Amberjon replied. "It reminds me of when Gramps taught me how to summon the dead. Except we were just faking it. If this is a fake, who's doing it? And why?"

Another voice spoke: "How can this be? There are no people anymore!"

"There are, I tell you. Look! I see three of them. Well, I'm not sure they're actually people. They're very strange-looking. But they all have bodies. How can that be? Where can they have come from?"

More voices joined in, coming out of the mist from every direction. They were soft and wispy, their words fading in and out, sometimes disappearing altogether.

"What do you suppose they want?" whispered one.

"I don't know. They seem to be searching for something."

"Why are you here?" cried the first voice. "What do you want from us? Haven't we given everything already? Why don't you let us be?"

A cold fear clutched my heart as we moved still closer together.

"Why do you have bodies?" shrieked a new voice. "It's not fair! Why should you get to exist when we cannot?"

"*Get them!*" cried another. "*Get them!*"

Invisible hands began to pluck at us. The feel of cold, unseen fingers pulling at my face nearly made me vomit. I screamed, and the assault stopped as abruptly as it had started. Trying to sound bigger and braver than I felt, I said, "Who are you? Why are you attacking us?"

"Who are we?" asked a deep voice. "Better we should ask that of you!"

"We have attacked no one," I replied. "You are the ones who should explain."

A vast and longing sigh, like the sound of cattails bending in the summer wind, rippled past us.

"We are the Petronians," said the deep voice I had come to think of as their leader. "And this is what is left of our world."

"What do you mean?" Lura asked. "What happened to your world?"

"It fell apart," replied the lead voice.

"Alas, Petronia. Alas, for the world that was, but is no longer," murmured voices all around us.

The lead voice spoke again. "This was once a mighty world. A solid world."

"We had thrones and dominions," added another voice.

"Castles and crowns," said a third.

"Rich farms and vast orchards!" added a fourth.

The leader spoke again. "There was a stone, a great stone of great power. It was the Heart of Petronia, the solid core of our existence. As the One True Story says, first of all things was the Stone. That stone, longing for a world, called to itself the swirling mists, which settled and drew together, creating Petronia. But now the Heart of Petronia has been stolen, so our world is no more. Without the Stone, we are nothing."

"Nothing!" echoed voices all around us. "We are nothing, we are nothing, we are nothing. . . ."

"It was the outworlder who did it!" cried a sharp female voice. "All of Petronia knows that. The outworlder came into our home with charming words and a lying tongue. Then he promised and cajoled until he corrupted the one who should have been our guardian."

"Death to the traitor!" cried a thousand voices.

"The traitor let the outworlder steal the Stone. Stealing the Stone, he stole our world, our lives, our very existence!" finished the female voice.

Shouts and cries—angry, heartbroken, forlorn—erupted all around us.

"When the world's heart was gone, Petronia itself began to dissolve," said the leader. "Then we did, too, falling apart until we became what we are now, lost souls floating in the void, floating in nothingness."

A wail of grief—not words, just pure emotion—rose around us. The ghostly hands attacked again, plucking at our faces, our hair, our eyes. Lura, Amberjon, and I drew together in a tight embrace, but the cold hands still pulled at us until I lifted my head and shouted, *"Stop!"*

To my surprise, they did.

"We mean you no harm," I said, hoping I was speaking

loudly enough for all to hear. "We are seeking the one who did this to you. He has stolen from us as well."

Murmurs of discontent and disbelief swirled around us. But the attack did not resume.

"We should start moving again," said Amberjon.

It was the only thing we could do.

For a long time the voices did not completely leave us, though the number seemed to dwindle. Every now and then one would grow bold and begin to pluck at us again. But all it took was a sharp command and that would stop. Then we began to dissolve, too.

19

BRAVE NEW WORLD

Lura was first to notice. Her cry of horror caused me to turn. I took one look at her bloated face and ice seized my heart. She prodded her right arm with her left forefinger. The flesh bulged and wobbled beneath her touch.

I looked at my own arm. It was thicker than it had ever been. I poked at it, and it jiggled.

I was coming apart! How had I not noticed this happening?

The voices began to mock us: "Look! It's happening to the outworlders!"

"It won't be long before they're nothing, too!"

"Won't that be a pity?"

Surprisingly, when we paused to rest we heard a new voice. From very close by it whispered, "I believe in you."

Speaking softly in return, I asked, "Who are you?"

No answer came. The voice was gone, or at least gone silent. Thankfully, the others had, too. Now that we were caught in the same fate that had doomed them, it seemed we were no longer of interest.

Now there was no time for sleep, and none for food. We pressed forward, fighting the mist and the gray with all our souls. If it hadn't been that each of us felt the pull of our stolen object, we might have given up. But there was no resisting their call.

"Concentrate," we urged each other. "Hold together. Sheer will can keep us safe for a time." But try as we might, fight as we might, our bodies grew less solid, larger, more loose. It was only a matter of time before we would join the bitter spirits of Petronia.

Making things even worse was the fact that the less solid our bodies became, the harder it was to move against the mist. Our only bit of solace was that ever and again that quiet voice would return when the others were silent to say, "I believe in you."

"Who are you?" we asked each time.

"Can't say. Don't want the others to know!"

We formed a meld while we still could, and that helped keep us together. And whenever the voices came we would lock our minds more tightly to keep them out. But we all knew the meld was fading, much like our bodies. How long could we maintain it?

What made the deadly slow pace of the journey even more excruciating was that all three of us felt the trail growing stronger. We could sense it from each other. So even as our progress slowed, the touch of the stolen objects blazed brighter in our hearts. Yet we had no way to measure the distance, or count the time. We might have gone a thousand miles. We might have gone six feet.

Madness crept upon us. We could not remember who we were, or what we sought, or even why we fought against dissolving. I knew only that something pulled me onward. And something inside me, some heartrending chance of loss, made it impossible for me to stop.

And then—one day, one year, one lifetime?—ahead of us we saw an orange sphere, pulsing with a life of its own, utterly different from the mist that surrounded us.

We made for it, not knowing at this point why we did so . . . only that there was nothing else to do, that we had no choice.

Drawn by the pull, one by one we entered it.

The trip through this sphere was the strangest passage of all. I felt as if I was being put back together out of pieces of nothing. I couldn't even say where the pieces of me had been. All I know is that when I stepped out of the sphere I had arms! And legs! And fingers and toes and all the rest of the things that go along with them. I had my body back! I felt warm sun on my skin and solid ground beneath me. And, to my relief, I saw the others beside me.

"That," said Amberjon, his hands shaking as he tried

to untie the rope that still bound us, "was the worst thing that has ever happened to me. And I speak as the survivor of a long series of bad things."

"Well, how do you think it's been for us in Petronia?" asked a voice from behind.

I spun around. Emerging from the orange sphere was someone we had never seen. The newcomer was short, about halfway between Amberjon's height and mine. It wore no clothes. It didn't need to, since it was covered from head to toe in reddish-brown fur. Only its face was fur-free. Even so, with its whiskers and extended nose, the newcomer's face looked as much like a cat's as it did a human's. However, it did walk on two legs and it didn't have a tail.

"Who are you?" I asked.

"Me? I'm Nuri. I've been following you."

"I recognize your voice," Lura said. "You were the one giving us hope as we traveled. Thank you for that."

Nuri smiled. "Glad to have been of service."

"But why?" asked Amberjon. "That's actually two questions, by the way. Why follow us, and why help us?"

"Because I could tell you were trying to do something important and because I had reason to suspect it was connected to the loss of my world."

"We said that more than once," I replied. "No one else believed us. Why did you?"

"Because I knew something they didn't."

"What?" I asked.

"Rather not say. Right now don't you think it would be a good idea for us to look around and see what kind of place we've come to? Stone and bone, it feels good to have skin again! Are you as happy as I am to have your bodies back?"

"Happy, and hungry!" said Lura.

"My stomach is so empty my belly button is kissing my backbone," put in Amberjon.

"Look up," said Nuri.

We stood close to a tree that was heavy with fruit— softball-sized purple globes that hung low enough for easy picking. However, the tree was surrounded by a low wooden fence. Beside the fence was a sign that said: ABANDON HOPE ALL YE WHO ENTER HERE.

I was trying to decide whether to climb the fence anyway when Amberjon said, "I'm not sure that's a good idea, Hurricane."

"Why not?"

"Look around."

I had been so startled by the cat-person's arrival, not to mention the fact of having a body again, that I hadn't taken stock of where we were. Now, following Amberjon's suggestion, I did look around.

I caught my breath. If we had just been through hell— and it sure felt as if we had—it seemed we had come out into paradise. Everything was so perfect that for a moment I wondered if we had died in Petronia after all and were now in heaven.

"It's beautiful," I said to Amberjon. "But what's your point?"

"It's almost too beautiful. Puts me in mind of an old story we have on my world. Let's just say that a perfect tree in the center of a perfect garden can cause . . . problems."

"That's odd," said Lura. "We also have a story like that."

"Oh," I said, pulling my hand back. "We do, too."

"Well, that's not the only tree with fruit," said Nuri.

The little cat-person was right. We stood at the top of a hill. Stretching around us in all directions was a landscape so serene and pure that it pierced my heart. I felt a strange sense of peace, longing, and fear, all rolled into one.

Clusters of trees, some covered with blossoms, others laden with fruit, still others tall and majestic, were separated by stretches of short grass. The leaves ranged from pale yellow to dark green to blazing scarlet, as if it was spring, summer, and fall all at once. Clear streams threaded among the hills, burbling cheerfully as they rushed over rocky beds.

I was still taking all this in when a soft breeze whispered by. Delight washed over me and my heart nearly exploded. It was a Windhorn breeze. The end of our quest was near!

The sun blazing in the clear blue sky was deliciously warm. Lura, Amberjon, and I began to shuck our heavy outerwear. Soon I was back to the jeans and T-shirt I had been wearing when I left Chicago on the back of a flying tiger. I pulled my sneakers out of my pack, then decided to stay barefoot for the time being. The grass was soft, almost silky, beneath my toes.

Lura was once again dressed in the simple shift and sandals she had been wearing when I first met her. She hadn't bothered to put on her cloak—the weather was far too perfect for that to be needed. As for Amberjon, he wore a light brown tunic that reached just past his knees. He had unwrapped his feet and I noticed he had only four toes per foot . . . which made sense, given his hands.

"Do you feel that?" Lura asked.

I paused, then realized what she meant. As one, Lura, Amberjon, and I pointed in the same direction.

"Let's go!" I said.

"We should pack up our cold-weather clothing first," said Amberjon.

I sighed. "I don't think anyone is likely to steal it. For one thing, it doesn't look as if anyone lives here."

"Well, someone put up that fence and that sign," said Lura.

"Okay, good point. But even if there are people, what would they want with these heavy clothes? This day is perfect."

"The day is perfect, but who knows what the night might bring," replied Amberjon, his voice more solemn than usual.

"Also, you shouldn't just leave stuff lying around," put in Nuri. "It's not nice."

So we packed up our things. While we worked, Nuri scampered around the tree, chasing a brightly colored insect. Or maybe it was a tiny bird. It was hard to tell.

When we had everything ready we shouldered our packs and started in the direction we had all agreed on. After a few minutes Lura said, "Nuri, I hope this won't offend you, but are you a boy or a girl?"

"Girl, probably," replied Nuri.

"Probably?" I cried.

"Well, yes. I won't find out for sure until it's time for the Change."

"What's the Change?" Lura asked.

"That's when I stop being a not-adult and turn into either a male or a female. You don't know what you're going to be until the Change comes. It's very exciting when it happens."

"Does it, like, happen overnight?" I asked, trying to imagine what it would be like to grow up that way.

"No, no. It takes a while. But once it starts, you sort of know what you're going to end up as. At least, that's what they tell me."

"Do you know what you *want* to be?" asked Amberjon.

Nuri shrugged again. "Depends on how I'm feeling. Sometimes I hope I'll grow up to be female, sometimes I want to be male. Lately I've been feeling mostly like a girl."

"But how do we talk about you?" Lura asked. "I mean, do you have a word for someone who isn't a he or a she yet?"

"Well, since I'm mostly feeling girl these days, you can

say 'she.' That will be fine for now. I'll let you know if it changes."

When Zephron told me we would be going to other worlds, I knew we would possibly meet people different from us. And Lura and Amberjon certainly qualified. But Nuri was beyond anything I had expected.

I decided not to say that . . . which I think indicates I was starting to get a little smarter. Instead, I went for a more important question. "How come you, out of all the Petronians, followed us through the sphere?"

"Amberjon already asked that. But if you must know, I was the only one looking for my father. I thought you might lead me to him."

"Why did you think that?" asked Amberjon.

"I would rather not say."

That annoyed me. I don't like secrets. But since I myself had plenty of things I didn't want to talk about, I let it go.

This was made easier by the fact that the world around us was wildly distracting. We were constantly exclaiming over some new flower, unlike anything any of us had ever seen. Or the warm sweetness of the air, which made you want to stop and just savor breathing. Or the fact that we occasionally saw animals in the distance, some graceful, some bizarre, some unlike any I had ever imagined when I was drawing fantasy creatures back in our apartment. After worlds that were windless, or drying out, or cold and dark, or lacking form at all, I felt as if I was being born anew . . . a feeling that increased every time one of those delicious breezes passed my way, seeming to whisper my name as it went.

We came to a stream and fell to our knees, cupping the water and lifting it to our lips. It was amazingly clear and pure. And it helped fill our empty stomachs.

"This is from Worldwater," said Lura. "I'm sure of it." She insisted we stop for a little while so she could wade in the stream. I was impatient—the pull of the horn was growing stronger—but I also understood.

Amberjon dropped down on the bank of the stream and said, "While you water your toes, Lady Blue, I am going to lie here and absorb this beautiful sunshine."

I filled our canteens, and we passed a happy few minutes breathing, basking, and bathing.

The peace was shattered by a shout from Nuri.

20

MOKURRA

"What's wrong?" I cried, wondering if we were being attacked.

"Nothing's wrong," Nuri said. "But look what I can do!"

That was when I realized her arm was buried up to the elbow in a tree trunk.

"Are you stuck?" cried Lura.

"No, no! I was careful. I started with just my fingertip and pulled it back at once."

I decided not to ask what she would have done if her fingertip had remained trapped inside the wood. Instead, I said, "Why did you start to begin with?"

"Um . . . it felt squishy?" she said, as if realizing for the first time that sticking her arm straight into a tree trunk might not have been a good idea.

"Can you get it out?" asked Amberjon.

"Oh, sure," said the cat-girl. She pulled her arm from

the tree, then shoved it right back in again. She did this two or three times, then said, "You try!"

Lura, Amberjon, and I each gave it a shot. The wood was completely solid.

"Can you do this with other things?" Amberjon asked.

Nuri walked to a nearby rock, stared at it for a moment, then thrust her hand straight in. "I have to think about it a bit," she explained. "But once I have it clear in my head, it's easy."

"Could you do that back in Petronia?" I asked.

"Not hardly!"

So . . . one more mystery about this mysterious new world.

"We should move on," said Amberjon. "The sun is getting low and I want to see what we can find today." Turning to Nuri, he added, "If you can teach me that stunt I will be eternally grateful. If by some miracle I manage to get back to my world, I will pack in crowds like the Circus Flamboyicus has never seen!"

The fact that he was thinking about making it home gave me an odd kind of hope. I was also, as always, hoping that the time peg was still doing its job. Was there a limit to how many worlds you could go to before it stopped working? I tried to shove the thought away.

We moved on. After a few minutes we saw something that, far more than the sign at the fence, made it clear we were not alone.

It was a building. At first sight it was disturbing. This

world felt so new and fresh that a building here seemed as out of place as an onion in a blueberry pie. But as we drew closer I saw that the building did not intrude on the perfection of the world. Instead it seemed to rise from it so naturally it was as if it had been meant to be there from the beginning . . . as if it had grown rather than been built.

"It's a temple," whispered Lura.

She was right. With its serene beauty, the structure couldn't be anything else. It was as graceful as a hawk in flight, and the sweeping curves of its architecture spoke of something deep and powerful. It stood on the shore of a wide bay and its far side extended directly into the water, as if to merge earth and sea. Slow waves lapped against its back.

We stopped a few hundred paces short of its doors.

"The horn is inside," I whispered.

"So is the fountain," said Lura.

"And the torch," agreed Amberjon.

"I hope the Stone is, too," Nuri whispered. "But I'm kind of scared to find out."

"I am, too," Lura said. "But we have to. *We have to.*"

"I agree, on both the fear and the need to enter," said Amberjon. "My armband is practically humming."

"I think we should leave our packs here," I said.

"Why?" asked Nuri, who wasn't carrying a pack.

I shrugged. "I don't know. If it's a holy place, which it seems to be, it just doesn't feel right to take them in."

"I agree," said Lura.

So we shucked our packs, then walked on.

The temple was fronted by a set of doors more than twice my height. Made of polished wood, they were carved with images of unlikely flowers and extravagant animals. Each door had a golden handle.

I summoned my courage, then stepped forward and pulled the handle on the right. The door swung open easily. As it did, a wave of warm air, sweetly spiced, rolled over us.

We stepped into an enormous chamber. Above us soared a domed ceiling supported by graceful arches. Beneath our feet was a polished stone floor decorated with swirling patterns. All the swirls led our eyes to the rear wall, which appeared to be made of gold.

In front of the wall was a boulder that I knew at once must be the Heart of Petronia. Resting on top of it was a fountain that *had* to be Worldwater. From it gushed a pair of streams that looked like liquid diamonds. The water cascaded to the floor, then flowed through channels carved directly into the stone to a pair of openings at the base of the back wall. I assumed the water went on from there to pour into the bay behind the temple.

Above the fountain two shelves projected from the wall. On the right, suspended in a delicate silver rack, was Spirit of Flame. The torch blazed with a fire that touched something deep inside me.

On the other shelf sat Aerobellan. My heart leaped at

finally seeing the great four-belled horn. At the same time I felt an ache for the Windlord and wished he was with us.

Attached to each of the stolen objects was a braided silver cord that extended to the top of the back wall. Who had brought these things here . . . and why?

I started forward, heading for the horn. But before I had gone two steps a wisp appeared, dancing between the altar and the four of us. I stopped and watched as the wisp pulsed and grew, emanating power. Soon it became a swirling cloud of dark colors—bloody reds, vivid oranges, bruised purples, and a thousand shades in between. In a deep, resonant voice, it said, "Welcome, travelers. I am Mokurra. Congratulations on surviving your journey through Petronia. I have been awaiting your arrival."

Panic washed over me. More than at any time since I had lost Zephron, even more than when we were in Petronia, I wished the Windlord was beside me. This being—this Mokurra—was something beyond my understanding. I sensed power and passion, and a mix of joy and aching loss so strong that for a moment I thought I might faint.

I waited for someone to speak, then realized that the others were looking at me, expecting me to be the one to say something. No one had elected me leader, but it seemed they had somehow decided that I was. Maybe it was because I was the first to start on the trail that had led us here. Before I could figure out what to say, Mokurra spoke again.

"I see that you are uneasy. Perhaps this will help."

The cloud swirled again, then began to settle. In moments it took on a human shape. It was still somewhat terrifying, since the shape was that of a fifteen-foot-tall man. Still, something about its human appearance eased my fear. Spreading his enormous hands, Mokurra said gently, "Better?"

"Yes," we all replied.

But Mokurra looking better didn't change the basic situation. I took a deep breath, then said, "I've come for that horn. I need to take it back to my world."

Mokurra's cheerful laugh should have made me feel better. Instead it chilled me to the bone. "Oh, but I need the horn here," he said.

"But it's not yours! Without it, my world will die."

"Without it, *my* world will die!" he replied, his voice like thunder. "Listen, and understand. You now stand on my world. I have constructed it with patience and tears, with agony and delight, and most of all with love. This is Mokurra's world. Its name is New Hope, and you are its first citizens."

Part of me wanted to hurl myself at him and start punching . . . which would have been absurd, given his size. Another part wanted to obey the panic that was urging me to turn and flee. As it was, I stood rooted to the spot.

"I should have figured it out," muttered Amberjon. "Gramps Branzancus taught me that four elements—

earth, air, fire, and water—make up a world. This monstrous flakbart has stolen those things from our worlds and used them to make a new world of his own."

"Very perceptive!" purred Mokurra. "This beautiful new world is indeed my creation. Using the elemental keys, I shaped New Hope with my own hands. I carved the rivers from the living soil and built the towering mountains, filling them with secret places. I made the plants. I designed the animals with care and cunning and love. Everything needed for a good life is here. You now stand in the Temple of the New Beginning, the first people to arrive in this perfect place, which will be your happy home for the rest of your lives."

That was when I erupted.

"Look, I don't know who you are, Mokurra—"

"No, you do not! You do not understand one one-thousandth of the tragedy that created me."

"Nope, and I don't care, either. That horn is mine and I want it back . . . same as Lura wants her fountain, and Amberjon wants his torch, and Nuri here wants that stone. We've got four worlds waiting on us to bring those things back to *where they belong,* and if we don't, those worlds are going to die. What kind of nut are you, anyway? You haven't got a single person here to use this stuff. What good is it? I mean, what are you gonna do with the whole thing? Give us back what you stole so we can go home."

I half expected Mokurra to smite me on the spot, or

blast me with lightning, or whatever it was someone like him would do. Instead he broke into booming laughter . . . which only made me madder.

"You are wrong on every point," he said when he was done laughing. "To begin with, my world is not without people. *You* are here! And, over time, others will come. I have ways of luring them, and testing them—just as I tested you with that trap in the world of the fountain."

"What have you done with Zephron?" I demanded.

"And with Belaquian?" added Lura, her voice trembling.

Mokurra rolled his eyes and waved an enormous hand in dismissal. "I haven't done anything with them. Belaquian left your world because you had nearly destroyed him, Lura. And Zephron simply abandoned you, Hurricane, dropped the quest when he realized he had no chance of retrieving the horn. You can't count on the gods or so-called protectors for consistency. They can be amazingly fickle. I, however, am not. I have been rooting for you to make it here and I didn't want gods and demigods along for the ride. What I wanted was people, real people, who could learn to love and worship me. As I followed your progress I grew more and more excited about your possibilities. When you survived your trip through Petronia you proved that you are the perfect first residents for New Hope. What better way to populate my world than to start with those who have the strength and courage and love to find it? One person from each of the worlds that contributed something to making this possible!"

He was so smug I almost expected him to start hugging himself.

"Something that is taken without permission does not count as a contribution!" said Amberjon. "Those worlds need what you have stolen from them."

"But those worlds were petty and ugly," crooned Mokurra. "Mine is beautiful, unsullied by hate, and therefore far more suited to live. You will be happy here. New Hope is the wonder and glory of the cosmos, clean and fresh, a realm of peace and harmony. And I offer it to you." Then, almost as an afterthought, he added, "Besides, your own worlds are dead and gone, and have been for over a hundred years."

That was when I fainted.

Actually, first I threw up all over his perfect polished floor.

Then I fainted.

21

"NEVER CON A CON MAN"

You would think that if you puked on the floor of a god—or whatever Mokurra was—he would vaporize you on the spot. Instead, I woke to find myself floating facedown a foot or two above the floor . . . which I noticed was clean again.

Maybe he smote the upchuck instead.

"I regret that I did not break the news to you in a gentler fashion," said Mokurra, sounding truly apologetic. Still talking, he somehow rotated me so I was back on my feet. "The thing is, your journey through Petronia took far longer than you realized. I understand that the four of you will need to mourn for a while. It is only natural. But it's not really such a loss, you know. I monitored your worlds carefully. You, Hurricane, must have been aware that Earth did not have much time left. Really, you people were shamefully careless with it! In only a few years the planet would have been heated to the breaking point and you would all have been dead anyway. I just moved the date forward a bit and saved everyone a lot of suffering. And you, Lura! What kind of world puts a mere girl on the throne of a god? There was a comeuppance due for that bit of arrogance! I don't need to go into all this. Each of you knows the flaws of your world. How lucky you are to have this one! So, yes, go ahead and mourn. But please try to keep it to a reasonable amount of time. Once you are done we can get on with the business of building New Hope. When you are ready, you may begin to worship me."

I snorted. You probably should not snort at a god, or even something that thinks it's a god. Once again I expected a smiting. What I got was a biff that sent me flying. It wasn't as if Mokurra physically reached out and flicked me away. I just felt a thud in my chest and found myself flat on my back, about ten feet from where I had been standing.

As I lay there glaring up at him and radiating a kind of hate I hadn't known I was capable of, he said, "For the time being I think it would be best for you to leave my temple. Spend some time recovering from your journey. Then wander my world. Sample its wonders. Soon enough you will forget your old, flawed worlds and learn to appreciate the incredible gift I have given you."

I was still screaming as we slid out the door.

When I say "slid" I mean exactly that. It was as if some

great force sucked at us, pulling us backward, away from that monster. The moment we were outside, the door slammed shut.

I rolled over and began to weep.

Lura knelt beside me and stroked my back, murmuring, "Hurricane, Hurricane," as if saying my name would change anything.

"You don't understand!" I sobbed. "My mother. *My mother is gone!*" Then I stopped myself, remembering that it was not that long since Lura had lost her own mother.

"We need to get away from here," said Amberjon. "We have a lot to talk about."

"There's nothing to talk about. She's dead."

"I'm not so certain."

"What do you mean?" I asked, wiping at my tears.

He glanced back at the temple. "Not here. Let's grab our packs and get away from this place."

"Which way should we go?" Nuri asked.

I was too gutted to answer, so I left it to Amberjon, who said, "Doesn't make much difference. Wherever we go, we'll be able to find our way back here anytime we want."

"That's true," I said. "In fact, I'm not sure how far from the horn I can stand to get."

"Let's go to the shore," Lura suggested. "Not right here where the temple is. But we can walk away for a while and then curve back down to the water's edge. I'll feel more at ease next to that much water."

No one had a better idea, so that's what we did. After

a while we came to a grove of trees that were covered with golden-yellow, egg-shaped fruits.

"What do you think, Amberjon?" asked Lura. "I know why you suggested we not eat from that fenced-off tree where we entered this world. But we're going to have to eat something soon and there's nothing in our packs."

Amberjon pushed down the tip of his long nose, which I had come to recognize as a sign that he was thinking. "Hard to say. I know a dozen stories that warn against eating in a magical land. On the other hand, I wouldn't call this place magical. Besides, if we don't eat this, what *are* we going to eat?"

"I'm starving," Nuri said. "But how can we know if the fruit is safe?"

"We can't," Amberjon replied. "But since Mokkie wants people for his world, poisoning the fruit seems unlikely. Boost me up, Hurricane, and I'll pick a few."

I cupped my hands so the little man could climb onto my shoulders. He didn't sit there, as I expected. Instead he scrambled to his feet, planting them on either side of my head. I staggered a bit at his weight but managed to stay upright.

"Circus training," he said, looking down at me. "Now grab my ankles and hold still. Lura and Nuri . . . catch!"

He started plucking pieces of fruit and tossing them down. When we had a dozen or so he said, "Okay, Hurricane, put your hands palms up at head level and then brace yourself." When I had done as he asked, he bent and put his palms against mine, then flipped over and landed on his feet.

Nuri and Lura applauded.

Amberjon took a bow, then said, "Who wants to try the fruits of our labor?"

"Let's all go together," Nuri suggested.

That made as much sense as anything, so we each took one of the fruits. They were sun-warmed and smooth, with a rich fragrance. I raised mine to my mouth and watched the others. Lura counted to three and we all bit down. My friends' faces showed what I was experiencing—unexpected delight. The fruit was juicy and utterly delicious. We tossed aside the walnut-sized pits, which separated easily from the flesh, then reached for more fruits.

"Better to wait," cautioned Amberjon. "We've been without food for a long time and we don't want to overwhelm our stomachs. Volcanic eruptions could ensue."

We grumbled but knew he was right. So we split the remaining fruits among the three packs, tucking them in gently.

"You look angry, Hurricane," said Nuri.

"I am! It makes me furious that someone as horrible as Mokurra can make something as wonderful as this fruit!"

Through the next few hours I pestered Amberjon to tell me what he had meant outside the temple. But he kept saying, "Wait till we settle for the night."

"The shore isn't much farther," said Lura. "Let's get there, then stop."

We bent our path toward the water and finally came through a cluster of trees with blazing red foliage to a wide beach kissed by gently rolling waves. To our left, far off along the curve of the shore, we could see the temple.

The sun was setting behind us, the day growing dark.

"I believe a campfire is in order," said Amberjon. "Both because I would love to have one, having been deprived for so long, and also because campfires have a way of helping people talk. Which we need to do!"

"Where do we get the wood for this fire?" I asked.

"An excellent question! I suggest we drop our stuff here and go back to those trees to see if we can find any fallen wood. I should have been looking for it while we walked, but I had other things on my mind. I hope Mr. My-World-Is-Perfect hasn't designed his trees so that they never lose a branch or twig. If he's really been thinking about having a population for this place, he'll know that people will need to use wood. If he's failed to understand this, we will be without wood but will know that he hasn't thought things out as he should. If he *has* understood it, we'll have wood, but it means he's even smarter than I think. I'm not sure which I prefer."

As it turned out, Mokurra was smarter than Amberjon thought and we were able to gather plenty of wood.

"Well, that was helpful but slightly disturbing," Amberjon said when we had the campfire set up. "Now let's see if my firestarters still work." He pulled the metal rods from his pack, held them above our pile of wood, and smacked them together. A bolt of flame shot into the wood. Minutes later we had a cheerful blaze to gather around.

Dinner consisted of more of the egg-shaped fruits. Though Amberjon preferred to eat in silence, it turned out Nuri was a bit of a chatterbox. Finally Amberjon gave in and joined the conversation. Holding up one of the fruits, he said, "These are delicious, but not enough to live on. Well, probably not. Who knows how much nutrition Mokurra might have packed into them?"

That led to a long debate about whether Mokurra had designed the animals of New Hope to be eaten.

Darkness fell and the sky was ablaze with more stars than I had ever seen, even on the journey to Zephron's cave. A huge moon rose over the water. Insects—at least, I assumed they were insects—sang sweetly in the distance. The waves lapped gently against the shore.

When we had finished eating, I said, "Okay, Amberjon, it's time. Tell me what you were talking about after we got dragged out of the temple."

"All right, here it is: I believe Mokurra is one big fat liar."

I felt as if I had been hit by a surge of the most wonderful electricity ever. "Do you mean my mother might still be alive?" I gasped.

"Could be. I hope so. All I know is that I don't trust him."

"Why not?" asked Lura. "And why do you say 'him'?"

"Aha!" cried Amberjon. "Why do you ask that question, Lura?"

She looked puzzled. "Because Mokurra is the most beautiful woman I ever saw."

"And what color was 'she'?"

"Blue."

The little man snorted and turned to me. "Is that what you saw, Hurricane?"

"No," I said, puzzled. "Mokurra was an enormous man dressed in white robes."

"And I saw someone who looked like me, except, well, big and perfect," said Nuri.

"Funny," said Amberjon. "I saw a tall man with a big nose and yellow skin. Understand? Mokurra appeared to each of us in the form most likely to persuade us to accept what it said. We were not seeing its true form because that's not what it wanted us to see."

"How did you figure that out?" asked Lura.

Amberjon smiled. "Never try to con a con man, my dear. I've been gulling marks since I was far younger than you. I sensed an uneasiness in that thing, saw something in its eyes that made me sure it was lying to us . . . and not just by showing us different forms! There's a deeper lie here. I don't know what it is, but I am as sure of it as I am of the four fingers on each of my hands. Mokurra is powerful, but also insecure, and a complete liar. The question is, *what* is it hiding?"

"I think I can help answer that," said a voice from the darkness.

Lura and I leaped to our feet.

Amberjon, perfectly calm, said, "Ah, good. I wondered when you were going to show yourself."

And Nuri, her voice full of hope, said, "Dad, is that you?"

A shape stepped from among the trees. As the newcomer came toward the firelight I could see that he was indeed of the same species as Nuri.

"Yes, dear," he said, "it's me."

Nuri burst into sobs and ran to him. Wrapping her arms around him, she cried, "Oh, Dad, I missed you so much!"

The cat-man held his daughter for a moment, then pushed her away.

"What's wrong?" she cried.

"I don't deserve your embrace."

"Why not?"

"Because I was the one who brought disaster to Petronia."

Nuri seemed to grow smaller. "I know," she murmured, hanging her head.

"But I did not do it for the reasons they think!" exclaimed her father.

"I believe you, Dad," said Nuri. But her voice was weak.

Her father looked around at the rest of us. "Will you introduce me to your friends?"

Nuri nodded, then turned to us and said, "This is my dad, Eklam Finstroth. Dad, this is Hurricane. This is Lura. And this is Amberjon."

Eklam put his palms together and bowed solemnly to each of us.

"Why do you say you were the one who brought disaster on Petronia?" I asked.

"Because I was the Protector of the Stone, and I failed in my mission. No, it's too simple to say I 'failed.' It was worse than that. I myself led Mokurra to the Heart of Petronia. But I did not do it for the reasons they think! I swear I had no idea of Mokurra's monstrous intentions when I led it to the Stone. I was simply trying to do a kindness. Oh, I should have known better. But Mokurra is a master of deceit."

"Exactly as I said!" crowed Amberjon.

"It presented itself to me as a wandering soul, survivor of a great tragedy, lost and lonely but filled with worldly wisdom. It said it was trying to understand worlds and how they are made. Even with that information I had no idea of its true intent. How could I have? Its plan was beyond my imagining!" Eklam shook his head. "I could sense power in Mokurra, though in reality I only understood a tiny fraction of how much it possessed. But the grief . . . oh, its grief was enormous and overwhelming.

"As Nuri knows, but it is likely you others do not, I was a priest in a position of enormous responsibility. It was my job to guard and protect the Heart of Petronia, the stone around which our world was formed. Every night I would travel the long tunnels and secret passages that led to its underground hiding place. Once there, I performed ancient rituals to honor the Stone. It was my task, and my sacred duty, to thank it for what it had done, and continued to do . . . provide us with a world and the chance to be solid upon it.

"Mokurra pleaded with me to let it see the Stone. Though I resisted, the waves of misery that radiated from Mokurra began to wear me down. And, I confess, it promised me great rewards if I would but let it see the Stone. Still I resisted, until . . ."

Eklam paused, and I could tell this confession was painful to him.

"Yes?" prodded Amberjon.

"I resisted until Mokurra showed me the story of how it came to be, shared that story in a link of minds that made deception unlikely because it was so raw and open."

Eklam was weeping now, and I had a sense that his tears were not only for his crime, but also for Mokurra's pain.

22

A VERY ODD GOD

Speaking softly, Eklam began his story.

"Mokurra's world was highly advanced and the people had a mastery of science that we in Petronia scarcely dreamed of. Alas, this meant they had created extraordinarily powerful weapons, as far beyond our bows and arrows as a mountain is to a pebble."

I felt my stomach tighten. I was pretty sure I knew where this was going . . . an ending that I understood was possible but doubted the others had ever even imagined.

Nuri's dad continued: "For many years they managed to avoid using these weapons. Then a leader who was bizarre and unstable, but gifted with great powers of persuasion, rose to high position in an important country. Within a year, he used the weapons." Eklam paused and I could sense the horror he felt as he struggled to continue. "When the insane leader launched his weapons, other countries retaliated. Soon more joined the battle. In less than an hour, their entire world was destroyed." He drew a heavy breath. "In less than an hour, five billion souls had lost their lives.

"But five billion souls snuffed out all at the same time do not disappear that quickly. In their terror, their loss, and their sorrow, they clung together. And slowly those five billion souls—souls brutally snatched from life and love and all that was good; souls seared by their sudden, ghastly deaths; souls filled with sorrow, and rage, and guilt—coalesced into one unbelievably powerful being. They became . . . Mokurra."

We sat in silence, too stunned by this story to speak. Finally I said, "So is Mokurra a god?"

Eklam frowned. "That is a question beyond my understanding. What is a god, anyway? If you mean a being of enormous power, Mokurra definitely qualifies. But it is also something new, something different . . . a godlike being created from a monstrous catastrophe.

"Mokurra has the power and strength of those five billion souls. But it is quite mad, addled by despair at the loss of its world. And it is at war within itself, a war between those who drove the world to destruction and those who tried to resist but failed. At night, I have heard it sob. When it does, wild rains fall from the sky. I have also heard it argue with itself. When that happens, the very ground begins to shake.

"You cannot think of Mokurra in terms of good or evil. It is the sum of every man, woman, and child of that lost world merged into a single being who is filled with awesome power and a heartbreak that is beyond understanding.

"Mokurra's all-consuming passion is to build a world to replace the one it destroyed, no matter what the cost, no matter how other people might suffer. It is like a god in one way: it longs to be worshipped and praised, because that is how gods build and sustain their power."

"Well, he . . . *it!* . . . better not be expecting to get any power from me!" I said. Then I looked over my shoulder, as if Mokurra might be standing there listening.

"Can Mokurra hear our conversations?" asked Amberjon.

"Or read our thoughts?" put in Lura.

"I don't believe so. If it could, it would not have needed me to lead it to the Stone—it could have just pulled the information from my brain. When it linked minds with me to share its story, it was a deliberate thing that I allowed. Even then I had no sense of it reading my thoughts." Eklam smiled grimly. "Given some of the thoughts I've had since then, if Mokurra could read my mind I'd probably already be dead!"

"Does it always stay in the temple?" Lura asked.

"No. Despite what it might have led you to believe, New Hope is not finished. Mokurra is often away, tinkering with the world's features."

"Tinkering?" I asked.

Eklam smiled. "Almost like a child at play, only on a

very grand scale. 'Ah! Let's try putting this mountain over here' or 'Maybe I should make this river a little wider.' That sort of thing. New Hope is definitely a work in progress."

"Does Mokurra know you're here?" I asked. "I don't mean sitting with us right now. I mean does it know you're on New Hope?"

"Oh yes. It brought me along when it stole the Heart of Petronia. That's why it doesn't consider me worthy of being one of New Hope's first 'citizens.' I didn't struggle to come here as you four did." He grimaced. "All *I* did was make this world possible by betraying my people. Mokurra put me in, oh, a kind of bubble until New Hope was almost ready. Once it was safe, it let me out, even though it could have kept me in that bubble forever."

"Why did it do that?" Amberjon asked. "Why let you out of your bubble?"

Eklam scratched behind one furry ear as if thinking, then said, "I believe Mokurra has a sense of honor, no matter how strange that might seem. It was keeping its promise to me."

"How long did all this take?" I asked. In the back of my mind I was thinking about creating a world in seven days and wondered if Mokurra had actually done that.

Eklam stroked his whiskers. "Impossible to say," he replied at last. "There is time as we know it, and there is what I can only call god time, where someone like Mokurra can work outside our normal flow of minutes, hours, and days.

It moved in and out of that time, coming back to our time to check on your progress."

"How do you know about all this?" asked Nuri.

Her father smiled. "Being a god—or a godlike being—is a lonely business, even if you are made up of five billion souls. Mokurra needed someone to talk to, and I was the obvious choice. Now, here's something important: Mokurra is not always here. I don't mean here at the temple, I mean on New Hope at all. Even in my bubble, I could always tell when it was away monitoring your progress. Things here were a bit . . . fuzzier. I suspect you'll feel it sometime, as I'm sure Mokurra will soon be off looking for more 'citizens.'"

"I have another question," I said. "What the heck is that tree with the fence around it all about?"

Eklam shrugged. "There's always a tree. There's always a fruit you cannot eat. Mokurra says it's one of the rules for every world ever created."

While I was letting that sink in, Amberjon said, "I have another question: Why is that temple so big? I understand the front part. It's meant to hold Mokurra's 'worshippers' once things get going. But what's on the other side of that back wall? By my guess the front section takes up only about a third of the temple. That leaves a huge area unaccounted for."

"I have no idea what's back there," said Eklam. "I don't know of any way in or out of that area. To be honest, I have never gone into the temple. I find it fearful, and do not think I would be welcome. However, I have walked the length of both sides, and even waded through the water behind it. There are no doors in those rear walls. Even if there were, I would not have dared enter. I am not as bold as you four."

"Speaking of bold, can you do this, Dad?" Nuri asked. Then she walked to a nearby tree and thrust her right hand directly into it.

Eklam's eyes went wide. "Of course I can't do that!"

"Then how come I can?"

Her father stroked his whiskers fretfully. Finally he said, "My best guess is it's because you dissolved with Petronia, whereas that never happened to me. Perhaps because our world is still dissolved, you are not fully solid yourself."

"Makes as much sense as anything," Amberjon muttered. "Now, if you'll excuse me, it's been a long . . . well, I can hardly call it a day. It's been a long whatever, and I am exhausted." With that he pulled some rags from his pack, wrapped them around himself, and said, "I'll see you in the morning. Assuming nothing else happens first."

Getting some sleep seemed like a good idea to me, too. I took out my blanket, then looked at Nuri. "You came here with nothing," I said. "Do you need a blanket?"

"Nope, I've got my fur to keep me warm. I'll just curl up by what's left of the fire. It'll be nice. How about you, Dad? You going to stay with us?"

Eklam shook his head. "It might not be a good idea for

you and me to spend too much time together. I worry that it would draw Mokurra's attention."

Nuri looked disappointed but I could tell she understood. Watching her watch her dad as he disappeared among the trees gave me a pang of longing for my mom. I saw Lura watch Eklam go, too. Then, with a sigh, she pulled out her own blanket, the one given to her back in the Cavern of Waters.

The night was warm enough that I didn't need a blanket to cover me. But it was nice to put it between me and the sand. I lay on my back and stared into the dazzling sky, listening to the waves roll gently against the shore. This world was so beautiful . . . and such an abomination. It was too bad I would have to do everything in my power to destroy it.

But what *was* in my power? Our power? What could the four of us do against a god, or whatever the frick Mokurra was?

I was still wrestling with that question when Lura sat bolt upright and whispered, "Hurricane!"

"What?" I asked, keeping my voice soft so as not to wake the others.

"It's Belaquian. He's here!"

I felt a tingle at the back of my neck. "Where?" I whispered, looking around nervously.

"I don't know! But as I was drifting off to sleep I sensed him calling to me."

I didn't want to tell her she'd just been dreaming, though obviously that was what had happened. She must have read my thoughts, because she narrowed her eyes and said furiously, "He's here, I tell you, here on New Hope!" Then she stood and pointed toward the temple. "He's in there!"

I managed to stop myself from saying, "It was just a dream." Which wasn't easy, since I was pretty sure that was the case. But I knew from the look in her eyes it wasn't something she wanted to hear at that moment.

Holding my tongue didn't do any good. Her next words were "You don't believe me, do you?"

"Well, it does sound kind of unlikely."

"As if everything else about this is perfectly normal?"

I had to admit, she had a point.

"So what should we do about it?" asked Nuri. She stood and stretched, clearly having been woken by our conversation.

"What *can* we do?" I asked. "We've been in the temple. There was no sign of Belaquian."

"Don't be silly," Lura said. "All we saw was the front portion of the building."

"So you think Mokurra is keeping Belaquian prisoner?" I asked.

"I don't know. I just know we have to find out."

"But did you see any way into the back area?"

"No. Wait! Maybe I did. Remember those channels where the water from the fountain runs under the back wall? Maybe we could get in through one of those." She paused, then added, "I should be the one to try, since I'm the one who believes that Belaquian is here."

"We can't let you go in there alone!" I said.

"Well, it would be crazy for us to all go. We'd be way more likely to attract Mokurra's attention that way."

"Lura is right," said Amberjon. Like Nuri, he had been woken by our talking. "What we need is some misdirection."

I scowled at him. "What the heck does that mean?"

"It means drawing attention away from what you're really doing. It's a major tool in the illusionist's workbox!"

"Could you explain that, please?" Lura asked.

Amberjon smiled. "Certainly. When I do a trick, I usually distract the audience by making broad moves with one hand . . . movements intended to hold their attention while I manage the actual trick with the other hand. You always want to keep the audience looking someplace *other* than the place where the real work is being done. That's misdirection. So . . . if we want to give you a chance to explore the temple, we need to draw Mokkie's attention elsewhere." He paused, then added, "The other option is that we just wait for the world to go 'fuzzy' the way Nuri's dad described."

"No," Lura and I said together. Then she added, "We don't have time for that."

Amberjon smiled. "I thought you would feel that way. So distraction and misdirection it will be. More fun anyway. My suggestion is that we split up as if we're going off to explore New Hope, just as Mokkie suggested."

He paused and began tweaking the end of his nose.

"You're thinking," said Lura.

"Yes, I am . . . and what I am thinking is that one of us should go back to that fenced-in tree. If anything is apt to draw Mokurra's attention away from the temple, I suspect that would be it. I wouldn't be surprised if Mokurra has put something there that will send an alert if anyone approaches it."

"Why just one of us?" I asked.

Amberjon rolled his eyes. "You need lessons in being sneaky, Hurricane! If you and I and Miss Nuri were to go off together, Mokurra would wonder why Lura wasn't with us and get suspicious. No, as I said, we should *all* go off in different directions."

"Okay, then I'll take the tree," I said.

Amberjon scowled but then said, "I would be inclined to wrassle you for that honor, but I think you're right."

"Why?" Lura asked.

"Because with his concerns about his mother, Hurricane has the most at stake, and is therefore the one most likely to contemplate the sphere as a way back. Not that any of us would voluntarily return to Petronia. But it would be a puzzle for him to ponder."

So that was it. We had a plan. Sort of.

We went back to sleep . . . sort of. I was too wound up

to sleep much, though I must have drifted off a few times, because I dreamed about my mother.

In the morning we had more of the golden fruit for breakfast. Then Amberjon pointed to the forest behind us. "I'm going to go that way. Nuri, why don't you wander along the beach. That will make it easier for you to find your way back here."

"I'm not a little kid, you know!" she cried.

"No, you're not. And it is entirely likely that Mokurra might come to talk to *you*, because you will be easy to spot, and because he knows your dad is here."

Nuri, who had been making an angry face, relaxed. "Okay," she said. "I can handle that."

"I'll take the tree, just like we decided last night," I said.

Amberjon nodded. "And I'll circle through the woods so that I am within shouting distance. I'd suggest doing a walking meld, but I'm afraid Mokurra might be able to sense it. I don't know what I can do if anything goes wrong, but I feel like I should be there. Lura, have you worked out what you'll do if Mokurra happens to be at the temple when you get there?"

"Yes. I plan to tell the monster I was curious and came back to learn more. I might even say you guys were mad at me for wanting to do that. Maybe I can get it to trust me. But that's my emergency plan. Mostly I hope the place will be empty so I can try to find a way into that rear area."

Amberjon glanced up at the sky. "Let's plan to meet back here at noon."

"How are we supposed to know when it's noon without a clock?" I asked.

Amberjon rolled his eyes again. "When the sun is straight overhead, that's noon."

"Got it," I said.

Then I headed for the tree at the heart of the world, wondering what I would say if Mokurra met me there.

MISDIRECTION

The tree was beautiful, the fence fairly ridiculous. I mean, the thing wouldn't begin to stop anyone who wanted to climb over it and pluck one of the fruits. Clearly it was meant more to warn you than to actually keep you out. Even so, the fact that Mokurra had taken the trouble to put it there made it intimidating.

I remembered Nuri's father's words: "There's always a tree. There's always a fruit you cannot eat. Mokurra says it's one of the rules for every world ever created."

What would happen if I *did* eat one of those luscious-looking purple globes?

I put my hand on the fence, half expecting to get some horrible shock. Nothing happened . . . at least, not right away. But while I was dithering about whether to scramble over it, Mokurra appeared, just as Amberjon had predicted. The sight of him—I couldn't help but think of Mokurra as male, even when he was in his cloud form—filled me with dread. But it was also good, since it meant he wouldn't spot Lura at the temple.

The first thing I had to do, something I had not prepared myself for, was to hold back from launching myself at him while screaming the foulest words I could think of. But that would be a bad idea, since he would probably just flick me aside and then maybe go back to the temple, which was the last thing I wanted. So I just stood there and looked at him. Well, okay, I didn't just look. . . . I glared. There was only so much I could do to contain the hate I felt.

The cloud swirled for a moment, then settled into the form of the handsome man in white robes. He was shorter this time, closer to eight feet than fifteen. Spreading his hands, voice almost tender, he said, "You don't want to do that, Hurricane."

"Do what?"

"Taste the fruit of this tree."

"Why not?" In this I was genuinely curious.

"Because with the first bite you will know things you don't want to know. Things you shouldn't know. Things that will never let you rest in peace once you do know them."

"But I come from a world where the fruit has already been tasted," I said. "We already know those things."

"Different worlds, different fruits, different knowledge," replied Mokurra. "There are so many ways for a man to fall from grace."

That was flattering, but I knew I was nowhere near being a man. I also knew that I could not match wits with a god . . . or the remains of five billion people who had become something like a god.

So I went for truth instead.

"I know you want me to love this world, Mokurra. But can you really expect me to do that when it cost my mother's life to make it?"

Mokurra's image wavered a bit, as if the monster was having a hard time holding on to it. Then he knelt and said quietly, "No, I cannot."

To my astonishment, I saw tears in his eyes. "I cannot, Hurricane. I cannot. But please know that I understand your loss, for I myself have lost so very, very much. . . ."

As the gut-wrenching ache in his voice swept over me, I realized that I was hearing the pain not of Mokurra, but of the five billion souls whose lives had been ripped away in the moments after the weapons of war were launched and their world was destroyed.

I didn't want to respond. I knew Mokurra was a master deceiver. I knew he was a monster. But that pain felt so raw, so real—and so much like my own—that it drew me to him. I felt the great losses of my own life—my father, my grandmother, and now, maybe, my mother—welling within me, an overwhelming wave of sorrow drowning my heart.

Mokurra reached out to me, grief calling to grief. I stepped forward. He pulled me into his arms and began to weep. I did, too. Together, we sobbed and sobbed and sobbed for all the things we had lost.

I don't know how long that went on before I pushed myself away and cried, "I hate you!"

"I understand that. But please do not hate New Hope, which I created to lift the heart and soothe the soul. Let me show you some of it."

Before I could object, I felt myself pulled into the air. Mokurra rose beside me . . . and we began to fly. Unlike when I flew on Shamoondra, there was nothing between me and the ground below. I would have felt like I was Superman, if not for the fact that I had no control over where I was going. Mokurra, flying along beside me, was in charge of that.

This was so much more than I had planned on when I offered to go to the tree! It should have been wonderful. Who hasn't dreamed of being able to fly? But I hated it, despite the exhilaration, hated it because it came from Mokurra.

Even so, I could not help but marvel at the beauty of what Mokurra had created. The hills and valleys, the forests and lakes were pretty much perfect.

After a while we settled to the ground beside a small

lake. Mokurra made a sound in his throat. Soon a pair of beautiful animals stepped out from the nearby wood. They were a little like deer, except their coats were shaggy and a gentle shade of yellow. They had large, dark eyes and long, furry tails. They walked to us with no sign of fear. One nuzzled up against Mokurra, the other gently butted me with its head. I stroked its fur. It was silken soft.

I didn't want to spend more time with Mokurra. I didn't want to be tempted to like New Hope. But I was afraid if I tried to end this, he would return to the temple and catch Lura snooping. So I walked with him along the edge of the lake while he talked about his dreams and plans for New Hope.

"There will be more people before long," he said, as if making a promise. "I'll be going off to recruit some soon. But don't fear—you four will always have a special place as the first citizens of New Hope."

I said nothing. Instead I kept an eye on the sun as it rose higher in the sky. Finally, when it was nearly overhead, I said, "Can you take me back soon? The others will be expecting me, and I don't want to make them worry."

Mokurra chuckled and said, "I will be glad to."

I hated how beautiful his voice sounded.

We rose into the air and flew back to the tree.

When I returned to the spot where we had spent the night, I was happy to find the others already there. I was especially relieved to see Lura, since it meant she had made it back before Mokurra returned to the temple.

"So, what happened?" I asked. "Did you get in?"

She shook her head. "The channels were too shallow for me to squeeze under the wall. But . . . I discovered a set of doors back there! We didn't see them the first time because our view was blocked by the Heart of Petronia."

"So did you get in?" I repeated.

"No, the doors were locked."

I sighed. "So there's no way in after all."

"I wouldn't be so sure about that," said Nuri.

I looked at the cat-girl. "What do you mean?"

She rubbed a furry hand over her whiskers. "Well, I could try going *through* the doors. . . . You know, the way I can stick my hand into things. If I can do that maybe I can unlock them from the inside. Then the three of you could join me!"

I looked at her in astonishment. "Do you really think you can do that?"

"I dunno, but it wouldn't hurt to try, right?" She frowned. "Or maybe it would hurt. I haven't gone all the way through anything yet. I should probably try to walk through a tree or something first, to be sure I can do it." She cocked her head. "I suppose it's possible Mokurra did something to those doors that would block me. But that doesn't seem likely, does it? I mean, why would it worry about someone being able to walk through doors? That's not the way things usually work."

"Why didn't you suggest this before?" asked Lura, sounding slightly peeved.

"You wanted to try your idea about the channels. Since you're the one who sensed that Belaquian is there, it seemed like you should get to be the one to find him." Lowering her head, Nuri added, "Also, we didn't know there were doors when we talked about it this morning. I was kind of afraid of going through a wall."

"Why would that be different than going through a door?" I asked.

"Because if there were no doors, I would end up on the other side all by myself! If I can let you guys in, that will be different."

"I think I can distract Mokurra again," I said. "I'm positive if I get near that tree he'll come back to make sure I don't go for the fruit. But we'll have to wait till tomorrow. I don't think I could pull it off again today."

"So the monster did show up?" Amberjon asked. "What happened?"

I hesitated. I didn't want to lie to them, but I also didn't feel comfortable telling everything that had happened.

"Well, I started by saying that I hated him. Probably wasn't the best way to begin, but I couldn't help myself."

"Weren't you frightened to say that?" Nuri asked.

"Sure! But then I realized my job was to keep him

occupied, so I got him talking by pretending I was about to eat some of the fruit. Funny thing was, he didn't get angry about that. Instead he got real serious and told me how much I would regret it if I ever did."

"So he threatened you?" asked Amberjon.

"Well, kind of. He didn't say *he* would do anything to me, like get all big and squash me under his thumb. It was more that he warned me if I took even one bite I would know things I didn't want to know, shouldn't know, and it would pretty much ruin my life."

"Sounds like a threat to me," Lura said.

"Yeah, it was pretty effective. Even if I had wanted to eat some of the fruit, I wouldn't now! Then he wanted to show me some of New Hope. Since it still wasn't anywhere near noon I agreed, so I could keep him away from the temple." I paused, then said truthfully, "Not just driving him away with my screaming rage was one of the hardest things I've ever done."

"Well handled," said Amberjon.

"Thanks," I said. But I felt guilty at the compliment, since I had left out so much of what had happened.

Now that we had a plan, the first thing to do was let Nuri try to pass all the way through a solid barrier. I confess I was nervous about it. . . . I had visions of her going into a tree or a rock and not coming back out, sort of like what happened with Zephron and the first Sphere of Passage. But Nuri was eager to test what she could do, so we trooped into the forest to look for a tree she would deem the right size.

"What, exactly, is the right size?" asked Amberjon.

"It should be wider than I am, so I can try getting my whole self through. But I don't want one that's too big, because what if I get stuck in the middle or something?"

I thought this caution made perfect sense.

When Nuri found an acceptable tree, we gathered around it. "Wish me luck!" she said as she squinched up her face and pushed one arm against the tree. It sank in without resistance.

"So far, so good!" she said with a smile. Moving slowly, she slid in sideways. When about three-quarters of her body was inside the tree, her hand poked out of the far side. It was bizarre to see parts of our friend sticking out of either side of the tree. But I thought I knew what she was up to. . . . She didn't want to be *entirely* in the tree at any point. Whether she feared that if she did she might not be able to get back out, or just found the general idea too scary, I couldn't say. As it was, I already thought she was braver than I would have been.

A moment later she popped out of the far side of the tree. We all cheered and congratulated her.

After that, time seemed to drag. All any of us wanted to do was find out what was on the other side of those temple doors. But we couldn't chance trying to distract

Mokurra a second time that day, so we had to wait . . . which was maddening.

We passed the afternoon seeking out different kinds of fruit. They came in a huge range of colors and shapes, and everything we tried was delicious. Even so, it was all . . . fruit. Finally I said, "If I do end up talking to Mokurra tomorrow, I'm going to ask what else there is to eat here! I never thought I'd be ready to beg for vegetables!"

"Make sure to ask if the animals are fair game," Amberjon said. He paused, then added, "I mean that in both senses of the term."

"Also ask if there are any birds we can eat," said Nuri, licking her chops.

Sleep did not come easily that night. I don't know how long it was after I finally did doze off before I was woken by someone shaking my shoulder. I sat up. By the light of our dwindling campfire I saw Nuri's dad.

"Mokurra is away," he said. "If you're going to try to enter the back of the temple, this is the time to do it!"

"How do you know Mokurra is gone?"

"Can't you sense it? The world is not as solid, not as defined as when he is here!"

I stood and felt the ground give beneath my feet. "I see what you mean," I said as I tried to catch my balance.

The sensation was frightening. Was this place likely to just come apart at some point?

After we roused the others Amberjon said, "How long do you think he will be gone?"

"Hard to say," Eklam replied. "He's usually gone for several hours, sometimes an entire day. Never more than two days, never less than a few hours. If you want to try this I'd say the sooner the better."

"Then let's stop talking and go do it," said Nuri. Then she added, "Sorry, Dad."

"No, you're right, dear. You should get going." He paused, then said, "Do you mind if I come with you?"

"Please do!" said Nuri.

Knowing that Eklam was the betrayer of Petronia, I wasn't sure about this. But since his daughter was the one taking the greatest risk and she wanted him along, I didn't feel I could object.

It should have been about a twenty-minute walk to the temple. It was made longer by the wobbliness of the ground. The way it bent and moved under my feet made my stomach queasy. I had to work to keep from barfing.

To my surprise, the outer temple doors were wide open.

"In case any of us has a sudden urge to come and worship him, I guess," said Amberjon. "Either that, or it's a trap. But I suspect not. . . . It's too stupidly obvious for that."

Naturally it was light inside the temple; Spirit of Flame, the ever-burning torch Mokurra had stolen from

Amberjon's world, ensured that. The only sound was the gentle splash of the water that fell from Belaquian's fountain.

Swiftly and silently we moved down the length of the temple, then around the boulder that had once been the Heart of Petronia. Since Mokurra was away our silence was unnecessary. Even so, it felt safer to make as little noise as possible.

The beautifully carved doors Lura had found were like a smaller version of the ones at the front of the temple. I tried both of them, figuring we should check again before Nuri had to try to pass through one.

They were still locked.

"Guess it's up to me," said the cat-girl, her voice a bit wobbly. She stepped up to the door on the left, closed her eyes, then pushed her hands directly into the wood.

"It tingles!" she cried.

"Are you all right?" her father asked in alarm.

"I think so. It was just a little surprising." Then she walked forward and disappeared through the wood.

THE ENGINE AT
THE HEART OF THE WORLD

"Dang," cried Nuri. "It's dark in here!"

"Can you find the locks?" asked Lura.

"I don't know. Give me a minute."

Finally we heard a cry of "Aha!" followed by a rattle and a clink. Soon one of the doors swung open. As it did, lights flickered on inside.

"Oh!" cried Nuri. "I wasn't expecting that. It's better, though. I can usually see pretty well in the dark, but there was no light at all when I came in here. None!"

The rest of us stepped into the temple's back area. It was huge, which we had expected. However, we found several things we hadn't expected. To begin with, the floor was not level. Instead, it sloped toward the back of the temple, which must have had some opening to allow the water of the bay to come inside, because the last twenty or thirty feet were completely submerged!

About fifty feet ahead of us stood another structure,

basically a building within the building. Its blue walls reached nearly to the temple ceiling. As far as I could tell, it had no windows or doors. What could it be for?

Between that structure and where we stood, some two dozen globes, each about four times my height, floated a few feet above the floor. These were not spheres of passage. Instead, they were the kind of globes you have in school, marked with seas and continents.

Amberjon was first to figure it out. "They're models!" he cried.

"Models?" Lura asked.

"Samples of possible ways for Mokurra to arrange his world."

Eklam nodded. "As I told you, it continues to revise what it has created."

"So this whole area is a giant workshop for designing a world?" I asked.

"It certainly looks that way," said Amberjon.

Scattered among the globes were a dozen or more tables. They were built to accommodate the slanted floor, so their surfaces were level. But they were too high for us to see what was on them.

"Boost me up, Hurricane," said Amberjon, going to one of them.

I obliged. Once he was standing on my shoulders and was able to peer over the edge of the table, he said, "Just as I suspected—three-dimensional maps! A good way to lay out smaller sections of the world." One other thing was especially noticeable about this section of Mokurra's temple: the braided silver cords attached to the elemental keys extended into this space, running along the ceiling, then disappearing into that strange interior structure.

"Well," I said, pointing, "if Belaquian is here, he must be inside that thing."

"He is," said Lura with complete assurance. "I can feel it."

We moved forward, careful not to touch anything. Part of me wanted to stop and study the globes, see the different ideas Mokurra had cooked up for his world. But even more, I wanted to do this as quickly as possible and get out before Mokurra returned!

But what did "do this" mean, anyway? What would we do if we *did* find Belaquian?

Given that doorless front wall, the first issue to deal with was whether we could get into the interior structure at all. "Should we split up, so we can examine both side walls at the same time?" I asked.

"Why don't I just go through the wall and see if there's anything in there?" replied Nuri.

"Are you sure you want to do that?" I asked, remembering her reluctance earlier.

"Yeah, I am totally up for it. Because I am getting angrier by the second and as we say in Petronia, 'Anger is strength, until it kills you.' I'm pretty sure I'm still in the strength phase."

Nuri's was clearly the better idea, and we watched as

the little cat-girl pushed her way through the wall. A moment later she stuck her head back out. "You guys have *got* to see this! There's no back wall on the place, so just go around and walk in. You're not gonna believe it!"

With Lura leading, we went to the left of the building and hurried along that side. About three-quarters of the way to the back we reached the waterline and began wading. By the time we got to the end of the wall, the water was nearly up to my waist. Amberjon and Eklam gave up wading and started to swim. Then we rounded the corner and saw that Nuri had spoken the truth: the back of the structure was wide open.

That was strange, but not nearly as strange as what we saw inside.

The first and most noticeable thing was an enormous stone slab, an oblong about twice my height that looked to be six feet wide and maybe thirty feet long. Like the tables, it was built so that despite the slanted floor, the top of the slab was level. The four braided silver cords stretched down to the end closest to the wall that Nuri had come through. Two more silver cords extended from the other end, down into the water.

As with the tables in the previous area, the slab seemed to be of a height suited for Mokurra to work at. Given that, it seemed odd to see a set of stone steps leading up the side of the thing. The steps ended at a wide shelf that stretched the length of the slab but was about three feet below its top.

Without a word, Lura splashed toward the stairway. The rest of us followed, dripping water as we went. I can't speak for the others, but as for me, I was both baffled and nervous. Before I knew it, Lura was sprinting. By the time I made it to the stairs she was already halfway up. She reached the top well ahead of me. Then she screamed.

When I joined her at the top of the steps I saw the reason.

Lying motionless on the stone slab, head toward us, was Belaquian.

His silvery-blue body—lean, muscular, and at least twenty feet long—looked as if it had been carved by a master artist. The braided silver cords that ran from the elemental keys were bound around his ankles, two on each of them. His arms were stretched above his head. Around each wrist was one of the silver cords that led down to the water.

I feared he was dead, until I noticed the slow rise and fall of his chest.

"What is all this?" whispered Lura.

For that I had no answer.

We moved sideways along the shelf as the others reached the top of the steps. Amberjon was next to arrive. "Belaquian?" he asked softly.

"Yes," replied Lura, still whispering, as if afraid to wake the sleeping god. "He looks exactly like the statue that stood in front of the Temple of Water. But what is this about? What are these cords for?"

"And who are these stairs for?" asked Nuri as she clambered up beside us. "Mokurra is plenty big enough to stand next to this . . . whatever."

"Future priests to attend Belaquian is my guess," said her father, coming up behind her.

"That would be my guess, too," said Amberjon.

"But he's a prisoner!" cried Lura. "Those cords are holding him!"

Before I could stop her she climbed directly onto the slab, ran past Belaquian's head, and grabbed the cord attached to his right wrist. I knew she intended to pull it off, but it was as if she had grabbed a live wire. She began to writhe and shake. Smoke curled up and silver sparks erupted around her.

There was only one thing to do, and it had to be done fast. I raced toward her and made a flying tackle. My speed and momentum yanked her free from the silver cord.

Unfortunately, there was no way to stop. We hurtled over the edge of the slab and plummeted to the floor. The water helped cushion our fall. Even so, we landed hard and it knocked the breath out of us.

"Are you all right?" I cried when I finally was able to speak.

Lura didn't answer and I was terrified I had acted too late. But after a moment she moaned and sat up.

"Are you all right?" I asked again.

She shook her head and held out her hands. Angry purple welts had been burned across both of her palms. I could tell that she was holding back tears of pain. "Well, that was stupid of me," she grumbled.

"Stupid, but brave," I replied.

"Thanks for breaking me free. But what do we do now? We can't leave Belaquian like that!"

Before I could answer, Amberjon said, "There's something else you need to see." He was standing a few feet away, out of the water, and had clearly hurried back down the steps. When we looked at him he added, "Glad you're both all right!"

"'All right' is an exaggeration," I said as I climbed to my feet. "I don't think I broke anything. But it sure feels as if I did!"

I reached down to help Lura up. She grimaced when I took her burned hand, but said nothing, which amazed me. I'm pretty sure I couldn't have been that tough myself.

"What did you want to show us?" I asked.

With a gesture for us to follow, Amberjon led us past the enormous slab that held Belaquian's body. Tears sprang to my eyes when I spotted what he was leading us toward. Tucked in a dark corner of this building-within-a-building, attached to the ceiling by a silver cord no thicker than my mother's knitting yarn, was a clear cocoon that dangled about three feet above the floor.

Inside the cocoon was Zephron.

The Windlord's arms were crossed over his chest. His face was blank but his eyes were wide open. Could he see us? How trapped was he? Suddenly I had a better understanding of how Lura had felt when she saw Bela-quian. Choking back a sob, I bolted forward, calling Zeph-ron's name.

He did not move. His eyelids did not flicker, his hands did not twitch. He looked more like a department store dummy than the lively little man who had dragged me into this adventure.

"He's as unreachable as Belaquian," I groaned.

"I'm not so sure," said Amberjon. He had a look on his face that I had come to know.

"What do you mean?"

The little man smiled. "Belaquian is clearly held by some horrible device. But this Windlord of yours appears to be trapped in something much more simple."

"Do you think we could reach him with a meld?" Lura asked.

"That's crazy," I said. "You can see he's frozen. Or co-cooned. Or whatever you want to call what Mokurra has done to him."

"Yes, his body is completely locked up," said Amberjon. "That doesn't mean his brain and spirit are not open for business. Lura's idea is definitely worth a try."

I couldn't decide whether that thought was hopeful or horrifying. The idea of Zephron locked unmoving in that cocoon but aware of all that was going on was appalling. Then I remembered that he had experienced something like this the first time Mokurra attacked him.

"So what are you suggesting?" I asked.

"First we form a meld ourselves. Then we put our hands on this cocoon, or whatever it is, and try to make mental contact with your friend. Three of us working together will have a better chance of reaching him."

Nuri and her dad watched as Amberjon, Lura, and I joined hands. We quickly reestablished contact with each other. Now the question was whether we could bring Zephron in as well. We put our hands on the cocoon and began calling to him.

Silence.

Silence.

Silence.

And then . . . an answer!

What a relief! Zephron said in my head . . . in all our heads. *I am so glad to see you, Hurricane! I have been consumed with worry on your behalf ever since I was brought here. How in the world did you get here on your own? And who are your friends?*

I introduced Lura and Amberjon and quickly explained how we had met.

Zephron, how can we get you out of this thing? Lura asked.

There is no way that I know of. But then, there is so much I don't know.

What do *you know?* asked Amberjon.

That we are in the grip of someone who is both insane and insanely powerful. Also someone who is a bit of a braggart, which is to our benefit as it means he has told me a great deal. Here is what you need to know right now. First, Mokurra will almost certainly be back soon. Lura's attempt to free Belaquian will have alerted him that something has gone wrong. But her instinct was right. Our best hope to defeat Mokurra is to free Belaquian, who is far more powerful than I.

But how? Lura asked. *When I tried it almost killed me. Do you know how we can break him loose from those bonds?*

I do not. But I believe I know how you can find out.

Hope flooded my heart. *How?* I asked.

One of you must taste the forbidden fruit.

The hope I had felt was immediately replaced by dread as I remembered my last conversation with Mokurra. *Are you sure?*

It is the only way. You will find the answer if you eat the fruit. There's always a tree. There's always forbidden knowledge. In New Hope, the forbidden knowledge is how to free Belaquian. Do you understand what has been done to him?

No, said Lura. *Please explain.*

Mokurra has harnessed Belaquian to the world itself. The four elemental keys are tied to him by those silver cords, which channel his life force. He is, quite literally, the engine that powers New Hope and holds it together.

So what will happen if we free him? Amberjon asked.

It will likely mean the end of this misbegotten planet. Beyond that, I do not know. Perhaps Belaquian can rescue at least one of our worlds. But there is little time to act, or to decide. If Mokurra catches you here, all is lost. If one of you is at the tree, Mokurra will go there first. Keep the meld! Taste the fruit! It is our only chance.

Amberjon, Lura, and I removed our hands from the cocoon but maintained the meld. It was strange to see Zephron frozen that way yet to have felt him so alive in my mind.

"I have to go to the tree," I told Nuri and her dad. "Lura will explain. I have to go now, and I have to go fast. If I can manage to taste the fruit before Mokurra can stop me, I may be able to learn how to free Belaquian. If that happens I will use the meld to tell Lura and Amberjon what to do."

"What will happen if we free him?" asked Nuri.

"It may mean New Hope just falls apart, which could mean the end of us, too. But we will at least have rescued a god who was made a slave. And who knows what he might be able to do if we can free him?"

"Sounds good to me," said Nuri. "Do it!"

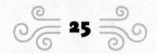

25

WHAT HAPPENED AT THE TREE

Dawn was breaking as I raced up the hill toward the tree. When I got there, I grabbed the fence and vaulted over. Before I could cross the distance from the fence to the tree itself, Mokurra shimmered into sight, once again in the shape of the tall man.

"What are you doing?" he thundered.

"Seeking wisdom," I replied, hoping he wouldn't strike me dead before I had a chance to pluck one of the fruits.

Hurricane, be careful! warned Lura.

Don't talk to me now! I shot back. *I can't afford to be distracted!*

Sorry, she replied, then fell silent. But I knew the link was still working. Which was good, because if I did manage to take a bite of the forbidden fruit and find the answer to freeing Belaquian, she would need to know immediately.

I hoped I hadn't betrayed what was happening in that quick conversation. Then I saw that Mokurra's face had changed. The rage was gone. When he spoke, I could tell he had decided to try to reason with me.

"Hurricane, I know you hold a fierce anger toward me. I understand that. I hope you also know I could end your life in an instant should I so choose. Why am I restraining myself? Why this mercy? Because I want no unnecessary death in my new world! That was my first rule in creating New Hope. I have had enough of death. And I still believe that you can come to love this world and claim your place as a First Citizen."

"I'd like that," I lied. "It's just that I'm so curious about what I would learn if I tasted this fruit."

Mokurra gave me a gentle smile. "You would learn a great deal about the truth of life and death. Not a good thing for someone who is both mortal and so young."

"I know a lot about life and death already," I said, thinking of when we lost my father, and then my grandmother, and of how even now I didn't know if Mom was alive or had been killed by the disaster Mokurra had created. For all I knew she had died before I even reached Zephron's cave. That uncertainty fueled my anger, which was good. I needed my rage to keep from giving in to the fear I felt facing this monster.

And I needed to taste the fruit so I could learn how to free Belaquian. But even if I managed to take a bite without Mokurra blasting me to smithereens, how long would it take for that information to appear in my mind?

Misdirect, I heard. Amberjon, of course.

"Would I become as wise as you if I ate one of these?" I asked, taking a step away from the tree.

"You might. But have you not heard the phrase 'ignorance is bliss'? You will pay a dreadful price if you eat that fruit, Hurricane. I do not say this as a threat, though my wrath will be mighty, and that is not a thing you want to experience. I say it as a warning. With a single bite you will know too much, far too much and far too soon. More than you ever imagined knowing. Will there be joy? Oh yes. But there will also be a sense of loss so wide and so deep that you will always be in danger of it swallowing you whole. You will never, ever be able to unknow the things that you will learn."

Misdirect, I heard again.

"Maybe if you explain some things I don't yet understand, it will ease my curiosity."

"That seems like a reasonable bargain. What is it you most want to know?"

What I most wanted to know was how we could free Belaquian, but that didn't seem like the best question to ask at the moment. So I asked something else, something that had been bothering me for some time. "How did you manage to bring the elemental keys here? They're pretty big."

My goal was to get him talking and slightly off guard so I could make my move.

Mokurra smiled, showing his perfect teeth . . . which, I reminded myself, were an image, not a reality. "An excellent question. The answer is actually fairly simple. I used my powers to reduce their size. Your Windlord's beloved horn fit neatly in my hand as I rose through Belaquian's mountain. I *could* simply have flown to the cavern. But that would not have left a trail for you to follow."

I felt so manipulated by this! "How did you know I would be following you?"

Mokurra laughed. "I didn't know it would be you, specifically. But I was confident your Windlord would come after me." He continued his boast. "I diverted him to New Hope when you went through the green sphere."

"Why did you do that?"

"I wanted you to come on your own, not with the help of a being of power. It was a test of your worthiness."

More fuel for my rage.

Mokurra continued. "When I took Worldwater from its pedestal I simply shrank it to a tenth of its regular size and encased it in a crystal box created just for that purpose. I did much the same with Doona's torch. And the Heart of Petronia was little more than a pebble in my pocket when I absconded with it."

"Your powers are amazing!" I said, partly to flatter him, partly because I truly was astounded by what he had just told me.

I hoped he had not noticed me tensing my legs to make a leap for the tree. It was a false hope. Face stern, Mokurra said, "Do not make me stop you."

"What would you do?"

"You can be replaced. I would hate to have to do it,

after you have proved yourself so worthy. But I have already begun to recruit others. You could be their leader, Hurricane—a priest at my temple, a position of high honor for one so young. All those things are available to you. But not if you taste the forbidden fruit. Not if you do that."

"Hey, Mokurra!" cried an unexpected voice.

In the second that Mokurra's attention was drawn away from me, I made my move, leaping to grab one of the fruits. As I did, Mokurra spun back toward me, raised a hand, and sent a bolt of power in my direction. From the corner of my eye I saw a flash of reddish gold leap over the fence.

It was Nuri's dad! He was the one who had shouted to draw Mokurra's attention . . . and now he had thrown himself between me and Mokurra.

The bolt of power struck him full-force. I heard a sizzle and saw Eklam fall to the ground, his furry body smoking. Mokurra cried out, in a mix of anger and despair. In that same instant, fruit in hand, I scrambled behind the tree and bit down. Bittersweet juice flooded my tongue, which felt like it was on fire.

Then the juice hit, and I feared my head was going to explode as that single bite opened a link from my mind to Mokurra's—Mokurra, who was made up of five billion souls who had been slaughtered when a mindless war destroyed their world in a single hour. Five billion angry, wise, hurt, loving, baffled, lost, and fearful souls who jostled and fought to be first to tell me their story.

So many stories! So many minds struggling against each other to try to reach mine! It was too much, way too much. I felt myself on the verge of passing out. But I had to stay with it, keep the Flow open, hoping to find the answer.

And suddenly, there it was! I understood instantly that it was close to the top precisely because it was the one thing Mokurra *didn't* want me to know. The very fact that it was the thing he was most trying to hide was like drawing a big red circle around it.

I had the answer and I sent it to Lura: *Kiss him! Kiss Belaquian! It's just like a fairy tale—a kiss will wake him.*

I heard a wail from Mokurra. My first thought was that it was because I had found the way to free Belaquian. I expected Mokurra to send another blast of power my way and figured that would be the end of me. But if what I had done could stop this madness, it was all right. If Lura could free Belaquian and my friends could get the horn back in time to save my mother, it was all right.

The blast never came. When I found the courage to turn and look, I saw Mokurra cradling the lifeless body of Eklam Finstroth against his chest. "Death has come to New Hope already," he moaned. "So soon, so soon."

He looked up, saw me watching him. I flinched back, thinking that now a blast of power would kill me as it had Nuri's dad. But Mokurra shook his head. Voice choking, he said, "You are safe, Hurricane. The fault lies with me. I am flawed, so very, very flawed. I was mad to think I could create a paradise. Not with what I came from. Not with what I am."

Gently he placed Eklam's lifeless body on the ground, then knelt over it, keening his grief and guilt.

I did the only thing I could think of. I crossed to him and said, "I know your story, Mokurra. I know it because Eklam told us. And I know it now because it lives within me. You warned me, you warned me not to eat the fruit. I should have listened, but I couldn't, and even if I could have I wouldn't have, because . . . because of my mother."

How could this monster, this mad demigod, who had thought nothing of dooming four worlds, be so moved by having killed this one weak and foolish creature who had betrayed his own world?

I knew. I knew because the answers were bubbling within me, the voices of the billions of souls who had perished when their world was destroyed. Not all of them. That would have been impossible. As it was, it was way too much, too many voices, too many cries of sorrow and regret. Mixed with them, even now, were voices that contained nothing but fear and anger.

As the voices clamored at me I understood even better how their world had died, and felt sick inside. And I also knew why Mokurra could do the things he had done to our worlds. Even after their world was destroyed, the struggle of these people had not ended. They fought *within* Mokurra, within his new form, voices of light and good crying out to do something better, to be something better . . . and voices of hate and fear, turning and twisting everything so that what might have been sweet and pure was sad and soiled and hopelessly, hopelessly broken.

As Mokurra bent over Eklam's body, I found myself remembering the last night my mother and I had spent at my grandmother's side. Mom had stroked Gran's back all through that long night, whispering, "It's all right. You can let go now. You've done your work, you've done your best. Now it's time for blessed rest."

I began to do the same thing for Mokurra. His back was massive and my hand felt tiny upon it. But I *knew* him now, knew him in a way possible only for someone who had tasted the fruit of that tree. I knew the terror, the loss, the pain, and the overwhelming desire to make something new and good to replace what had been lost.

"It's all right," I crooned, repeating my mother's words from that long-ago night. "You can let go now. You've done your work, you've done your best. Now it's time for blessed rest." Then I added words of my own. "You warned me that if I ate the fruit I would know more about life and death than was good for me. And you were right, Mokurra. You were so right. But because I did, I can tell you what I have learned. Death is not the end, and it is not the enemy. It comes to us all, and it is just part of the deal, part of the price of the joy of being alive to begin with. You can let go now. You've done your work, you've done your best. Now it's time for blessed rest."

And because I knew him, knew him in a way that was frighteningly intimate, I felt it when something inside him let go. I wasn't telling him anything he didn't know, and a part of him was fighting it, struggling to hold on. But the greater part—and, I like to believe, the better part—seized on my words.

And then . . . he began to come apart.

How can I describe this? At first it was as if tiny sparks were rising from him. For a moment I was afraid he was actually going to catch fire. Then the shape that he used when presenting himself to me, that of the beautiful giant in white robes, began to shimmer. Seconds later he became once more the swirling cloud of angry colors that had confronted us in our first moments in the temple.

I fell back, terrified that the anger was winning now. But the colors calmed, gentled. More and more sparks rose and drifted away, a spray, and then a fountain, and then a cascade, like an upward-flowing waterfall made of a million . . . a billion . . . five billion tiny points of light as Mokurra swirled toward the sky and disappeared.

His better side had won at last.

WORLDQUAKE

As when Mokurra was away, the ground grew soft and spongy. Did this mean the world would simply grow less solid with Mokurra gone? Or did it mean New Hope was going to completely fall apart?

I had lost contact with Lura and Amberjon shortly after I sent the message about how to wake Belaquian. Now I could sense them battling against the other voices in my head to reconnect with me. But the babble was too much and they weren't able to get through. I could barely think but somehow managed to realize I needed to get back to the temple.

I had only gone about halfway down the hill when I heard a rumble. I figured that what I had feared was coming true: New Hope was falling apart.

I was wrong . . . what was falling apart just then was Mokurra's temple.

More precisely, it was being *blown* apart. Belaquian

had burst through its roof! Pieces of it flew in all directions as the enormous form of the water god leaped over the shattered walls. In his arms he clutched the Heart of Petronia. Carrying the boulder as if it weighed no more than a feather, Belaquian raced up the hill, then flung the enormous stone through the orange sphere that still pulsed near the tree.

Threw it back into Petronia.

Without the Heart of Petronia, the elemental key that was the source of all that was solid, Mokurra's world did start to crumble. The ground shuddered and shook beneath my feet as great fissures extended out from the base of the tree.

My heart clenched. I had been prepared to die when I challenged Mokurra. Having survived that, I didn't want to die on this dying world. I wanted to get back to my mother!

Then I saw something that lifted my heart. Zephron had emerged from the ruins of the temple . . . and he was carrying the horn! It was enormous, and I realized again that he must be stronger than he looked. Behind the Windlord came Amberjon, holding aloft Spirit of Flame. A moment after that it was Lura, clutching a crystal cube that I was sure must contain Belaquian's fountain, now shrunken again as Mokurra had described. Scampering alongside her was Nuri.

I felt a wave of grief as I realized the little cat-girl did not yet know that her father was dead.

I turned again. Belaquian stood by the tree, his eyes closed, his body trembling with effort. The quaking world grew still for a moment and I realized that—once again—he was the force holding it together. But I could also see that the effort was draining him and could not go on for long.

As Zephron drew close to the top of the hill he cried, "I don't know what you did, Hurricane, but whatever it was, it was well done. Now follow me!" With those words he flung himself, horn wrapped around him, into the orange sphere.

I shuddered at the thought of returning to Petronia . . . but the alternative was to stay here on a world that was about to tear itself apart.

"Don't just stand there!" shouted Amberjon as he raced past. Carrying the torch, whooping with triumph, he leaped into the orange sphere.

"Come on, Hurricane!" urged Lura.

But the multitude of voices unleashed by the forbidden fruit were still confusing me and I just stared stupidly as Lura, too, entered the sphere.

It was only when Nuri grabbed my hand, tugged at it, and cried, "Belaquian can't hold this place together forever!" that I broke free of my stupor and started to move. We had only gone a few paces when she stopped and wailed, "Dad!"

The world shook beneath our feet. Belaquian groaned with the struggle of holding it together. But Nuri broke free of my hand and ran to her father's body, crying, "Dad! Dad!" Shaking with sobs, she threw herself over his corpse.

I made my way to her, scarcely able to walk across the unstable ground. "He sacrificed himself to save me," I said. "To save all of us."

A crevice broke open not three feet past us. "Nuri, we have to go!" I said.

"You go!" she sobbed, her face buried against her father's chest.

Knowing she wouldn't leave him, I knelt and gathered Eklam's body into my arms. "Now come on!" I said. "Your world needs you."

Nuri wiped at her eyes, then got to her feet. The ground shook again. I staggered, still disoriented by the voices that continued to clamor in my head.

At that moment, I felt Zephron's arm around me. He had come back to get me! "We have to go, Hurricane," he said gently but firmly.

With his support, still carrying Eklam's body, I stumbled as fast as I could toward the sphere, counting on Nuri to follow. I hesitated at the edge and looked back. Belaquian saw me, nodded, and said, "That was well done. All of it. *Now go!*"

Then he lowered his arms. Instantly, New Hope began to shred itself. The tremors grew threefold. Mighty trees fell sideways and crashed to the ground. The sound of grinding rocks was deafening. Great crevices split the world, then slammed shut as other, even bigger ones yawned open. A huge rift, too wide for me to leap while holding Eklam, opened at my feet. I staggered, nearly fell in, but Zephron grabbed my arm and pulled me back. The rip in the ground grew wider.

Then Belaquian swooped overhead and the wake of his passing pulled Zephron, Nuri, and me into the orange sphere, back to the nothingness of Petronia.

From behind I heard a massive explosion as Mokurra's stolen paradise collapsed in on itself, then vanished.

We were in the mists again, with Amberjon's torch providing a weird, flickering light.

Floating in nothingness is not so bad when you have a twenty-foot-tall silvery-blue god beside you. But if Belaquian's presence reduced our fear, it did nothing to assuage Nuri's grief. I had released my hold on her father. Now Eklam's lifeless body hung suspended in the mist with the rest of us. Nuri clung to him, weeping bitterly.

"Your father made it all possible, Nuri," I said. "He distracted Mokurra to give me a chance to pluck one of the fruits. When I dove for the tree, your dad threw himself in front of the blast of power Mokurra sent to stop me. If he hadn't done that, I would have been dead before I could take a bite and find out how to free Belaquian."

"He was a hero," said Lura gently, stroking Nuri's back, much as I had stroked Mokurra's.

"I know," said Nuri, wiping at her eyes again. "And I know he would have wanted it this way, because he felt so guilty about what he had done. Even so . . ."

Her voice broke, and she buried her face against her father's neck.

After a while Amberjon turned to Belaquian and said softly, "So, boss, thoughts about what to do next? I'm kind of hoping we're not going to have to make the trip back across Petronia the long, slow way."

I had been averting my eyes so as not to look at Belaquian directly. You want to be careful around a god. But the warmth of his chuckle in response to Amberjon's question drew my gaze to the water god's face. He truly was awesome, yet I saw great kindness in his expression. Feeling bolder, I said, "Can I get a few answers before we move on?"

"That is the least I can do for you, considering what you risked and what you accomplished. I have some questions for you as well, but you may go first."

"Well, mostly what I want to know is what happened in the temple after I gave Lura the message that a kiss should wake you."

What I really meant, though I didn't want to say it right out, was "What took you so long to get to me after that?"

The first part of the answer came from Lura. "You were

right about a kiss," she said. "But even though it woke Belaquian, it didn't break those silver cords."

"I was struggling against them, but they would not yield," said Belaquian. "Then, without a hint that it was about to happen, they simply vanished."

"As did that cocoon in which I was imprisoned," put in Zephron. "It dumped me to the floor. My landing was undignified, but I was glad enough to be free. I assume that this all happened when Mokurra disappeared."

"I am sure that is correct," said Belaquian. "But how in the world did you do that? What happened?"

Though it seemed odd to be explaining something to a god, I took a breath, then told my story.

It left the others staring at me with wide eyes.

"That was well done," Belaquian said at last. "Well done indeed."

The admiration I heard in his voice filled me with pride.

The water god turned to Nuri. "Little one with the broken heart, I have an offer for you. Now that we have returned the Heart of Petronia, your world will slowly regain its form. Eventually it will be healed and all that was will once more be. However, this restoration will not happen quickly, and I do not think it would be good for you to stay here while it does. I am going to ferry your friends back to the sphere where they entered. I think you should come with us."

"You can stay in my world if you want," said Amberjon

gently. "You would be a big attraction at the Circus Flamboyicus! And I would make sure you were treated well."

Nuri shook her head. "Thank you, Amberjon. I would like to be with you, but I don't think I would want all those people gawking at me."

"I take your point," said Amberjon.

Belaquian smiled. I had never imagined how dazzling it would be to see a god smile. "Let me suggest you continue on to my world, Nuri. You will be welcome in the Cavern of Waters and we will give your father's body all due honors for the service he has rendered. And I will give you some training, because as your world begins to reassemble itself, it is going to need you to take his place as Protector of the Stone."

"Thank you," said Nuri.

Turning to Zephron and me, Belaquian said, "And I will help speed your passage on from my world, of course. Now, if you're ready . . ."

Our first journey across Petronia had seemed to take an eternity. The return trip, trailing in the wake of a god, took but minutes. We let out a cheer when we saw the first sign of the blue sphere through which we had entered. Belaquian paused, hovering just outside it, then said, "You should go first, Amberjon." Then he gave the little man a gentle nudge with one enormous finger. Spirit of Flame flickered with the forward motion as Amberjon vanished into the sphere. The rest of us followed, Belaquian bringing up the rear.

I was amazed when I stepped into the cave to see that the torch's flame had doubled in size.

"Who's there?" Doona called. "Amberjon, is that you? Have you come back?"

"Indeed, my lady, I have returned and brought Spirit of Flame with me!"

We started for the main cave. The passage was low, and I looked behind to see how Belaquian would manage it. To my surprise, he was now less than half the height he had been.

"Well, that's a pretty good trick," Lura whispered.

"Must be handy being a god," I replied.

Doona's face shone with a radiant joy and tears sparkled on her cheeks. And she was not alone. Surrounding her, looking both astonished and delighted, were five women and three men, all about Amberjon's size. I was pretty sure each would be wearing an armband like the one Amberjon had on.

Without a word, the little people surged forward and lifted Amberjon until he was high enough to step onto the altar. His face solemn and reverent, he thrust the base of the torch into the altar. Instantly, Spirit of Flame blazed even brighter. A gentle warmth flooded the cave. And with a sigh of relief, Doona rose from her chair.

I watched in wonderment as her lank hair grew thick, turning from white to pale gold. Years seemed to drop from her face. Kneeling in front of Belaquian, she murmured, "Thank you for returning life to my world."

The water god reached down, put a hand under her chin, and drew her to her feet. "It was not me alone. Each had a part to play. I could do nothing until they freed me."

"We need to keep moving," I whispered to Zephron. "We have to get back!" It felt rude, but I was desperate to return the horn to our own world.

"Remember the time peg," he replied. "Now that all has been settled we'll get back at the very moment we left. No time will be lost."

I believed him, mostly. But that did nothing to curb my impatience. Besides, there was no time peg in Lura's world, so we needed to get the fountain back there as quickly as possible. Despite Doona's pleading for us to stay for a while, we had to move on . . . though without Amberjon.

I hadn't known the little man all that long. But once you've been in the meld with someone it feels as if you've known them forever. Now that it was time to leave, I felt a stab of sorrow as I realized how much I was going to miss him.

"Don't forget misdirection," he whispered in my ear as I hugged him good-bye. "You can get away with a lot once you know how to use it!" He winked at me and smiled the smile of a rogue.

"I'll remember," I promised.

Then I turned to wipe away some tears while Lura and Nuri made their good-byes.

As we stepped out of Doona's cave I saw a rosy dawn spreading across the sky. Belaquian put his arms above his head, stretched upward, and returned to his regular size. Without warning, he swooshed into the air and we were flying again, this time over solid ground. As we passed above the village where we had met Amberjon we saw that the people were capering in the street, singing their happiness at the return of light.

Then, so fast it made my head spin, we were back at the scarlet sphere that led to the Cavern of Waters.

Because the sphere brought us out in an area well behind the main cavern, at first no one realized we had returned. That didn't last long. When we walked into the central area our arrival caused an eruption of joy unlike anything I had ever seen. Shouting, screaming, weeping, laughing, the cavern dwellers swarmed around Belaquian, clamoring to know what had happened and how he had managed to return. Well, most of them went to Belaquian. Urbang came leaping to my side, her grin so wide I feared her head would split.

Before I could greet her, Belaquian called for silence. "I will answer your questions in due time," he told the throng, in a voice that brooked no denial. "First I have work to do!"

The god of water strode to the pedestal that had once held the fountain, then placed his enormous hands on the torn and twisted surface. The platform began to glow, and even though it was made of stone, I saw it melt and flow beneath his fingers. Soon the places where it had been damaged when Mokurra wrenched the fountain loose were healed and smooth.

Belaquian turned to Lura. "The fountain, please."

Smiling, she held up the crystal box. Belaquian took it from her, raised the lid, and gently lifted out the tiny fountain. It glimmered, then began to grow. He placed the fountain atop the platform. It continued to grow. Moments later it was full-sized. A cheer erupted as water spurted up and out. The crystal cascade quickly filled the granite basin, then flowed over the edge into the channels that led to the waterfall at the mouth of the cavern.

"Now," said Belaquian, turning to me and Zephron, "we must send you two home in the swiftest way possible, as things are surely hanging by a thread there as well. Then Lura and I have work to do."

"You'll let me stay?" Lura asked. "After all I've done to you?"

"The damage was caused by Solarian, my dear, not you. What *you* did was rescue me."

"How did Mokurra capture you to begin with?" I asked. "I mean, you're pretty powerful."

"Not as powerful as I once was. When the people turned away from me, my powers diminished. That was not entirely bad. Worlds must outgrow their gods eventually. But this left me weakened when Mokurra came. Also, he took me by surprise, because . . . well, who would ever have expected someone like Mokurra?"

Belaquian turned back to Lura. "It's not just that I want you to stay. It's that I *need* you to stay. It's time to prepare you to take my place."

Her eyes widened. "Take your place?"

Belaquian smiled. "I must leave sometime soon. Another world, younger than this, will be needing me. And who better to take my place in this one than my daughter?"

That was when Lura fainted . . . something for which I could not blame her. I mean, what are you supposed to do when you find out that your dad is a god? Fainting seemed like the best option.

Of course, no one could let that be and give her a chance to rest. Kartanga, who had felt such anger at her when he first met her, knelt behind her and gently lifted her head into his lap. Looking up at Belaquian, the frog-man said in a puzzled voice, "But all those times at the viewing pool that we saw her mother, and then her . . ."

"Did you ever hear me speak of them in anger?" replied Belaquian.

Kartanga blinked. "No. I just thought . . ."

"Peace," said Belaquian. "I was simply checking on her, and also showing you what was happening, why I was growing weaker. Everything else was in your own thoughts."

Opening her eyes, Lura looked up at Belaquian. "Did you say what I think you said?"

The water god did something lovely. He shrank to human size, lifted Lura in his arms, and said, "Yes, daughter, I did. I have longed to bring you to me for years now. But your mother wanted to keep you with her, which I understood. After her death I was working on how best to reveal myself to you. Alas, before I could manage that, I faced the unexpected arrival of Mokurra. You need to understand that I am not meant to stay in power here forever. In time I must move on, as have the gods in Nuri's world, and Hurricane's. You, as my child, will be the Guardian of Water. You'll be coming into your powers soon—in fact, that has already started. It was why you could sense my presence in New Hope."

"But . . . you'll teach me, right? You must do that, at least."

"Naturally. And when you are ready, we will go together to deal with Solarian." He smiled that radiant smile. "A task that should be fun. But our immediate job is to get your friends home as quickly as possible."

He turned to Zephron and me. "Are you ready?"

"Um, not quite," I said.

Zephron looked at me in puzzlement.

"If we're going back the way we came, I don't think there's any way we can bring the horn with us. There's a cliff we'll need to climb down, and . . ."

Belaquian threw back his head and laughed. "Are you asking if I can shrink the horn, the way Mokurra did when he stole it?"

"Well, yes . . . but only if there is a way to make it grow again once we get it back!"

"Consider it done," Belaquian said. He returned to his regular size, then took the horn in his massive hands and stared at it. I watched in wonder as it shrank to the size of a soccer ball. He handed it to Zephron, then bent low and whispered in the Windlord's ear. I was dying to know what he said, but you shouldn't get too pushy with a god. After a moment Zephron nodded and said, "Good. I can do that."

Belaquian turned to me again. "Now are you ready?"

"The sooner the better!" I cried.

part three

WHAT DREAMS
MAY COME

27

WIND MUSIC

Zephron and I stood beside the basket that would lower us to the base of the mountain, the Windlord clutching the shrunken horn as if he would never let it go.

Eager as I was to be on our way, I felt a painful tug in my heart. In a fairly short time Lura and Nuri and I had gone through more trials and dangers and general weirdness than most people experience in a lifetime. Now that the moment had come to say good-bye to them, I wasn't prepared for the sorrow that overcame me.

Though we were not in a meld, Lura read my mind. "I know," she whispered. "I know." She opened her arms and we hugged each other, hugged hard, painfully aware it would probably be the last time ever.

Nuri stood waiting, and when Lura and I broke our embrace she said, "I wish you could stay. I wish you could be my big brother!"

I smiled. "And I wish you could be my little . . . sister?"

She giggled. "Probably your sister. I don't have to decide yet." I squatted down and she put her furry arms around my neck. "Thank you for not leaving me and my father in New Hope," she whispered.

I shook my head. "I never would have done that in a million years."

I gave her a final hug, then stepped into the basket.

"When you reach the bottom, pick one of the smaller boats," said Belaquian. "Once you have it ready to go, tug on the rope. That will be my signal to direct the waters. Though the lake is still filling, I will create a current that will speed you across its center, then downstream to the point where you entered our world."

"Thank you," Zephron said.

"It is the least I can do," replied the water god.

Zephron passed Aerobellan to me, then climbed into the basket. I handed the horn back and climbed in beside him. I gave a farewell wave to Lura, and the Water People started to turn the cranks.

We had descended only a few feet when the lights came on. Zephron exclaimed in wonder at the artwork that encircled us.

At the bottom we quickly found a small boat that seemed right for the two of us. Zephron tugged on the rope attached to the basket. It lifted away from us and disappeared into the now-dark shaft.

A moment later the water in the cave began to rise. As it swirled up we pushed the little craft into the current and clambered aboard. The boat was equipped with oars, but we had no need of them. The water—moving, I was sure, at Belaquian's command—lifted us and we shot from the cave into the lake bed. The water in the lake had risen, but it was far from full. That made no difference to Zephron and me. We were riding a surging stream about ten feet wide that rushed through the center of that great earthen bowl.

I've never been to Disney World—or any theme park, for that matter. All I can say is if anyone could create a ride like this I think they'd make a fortune. The water rolled and roiled beneath us and we hurtled forward at breathtaking speed. As the landscape flashed past, I recognized places from my long walk to the cliffs. Zephron and I shouted and laughed as the boat rocked and bucked yet never seemed in danger of overturning.

In less time than I would have thought possible, we barreled past the abrupt wall of trees that marked the beginning of the forest. Slowly the flow of the water grew calmer, but no less swift. It wasn't long before we passed the place where I first met Urbang. I smiled then, knowing we were close to a hill that held a cave with a strange green sphere inside.

It was clear that Belaquian was still guiding the flow, because when we reached the best spot for it, the boat diverted to the bank of the river. Moments later Zephron and I were hurrying up the hill, the Windlord moving at a speed you would have thought impossible for someone as old as he appeared to be. I led the way, of course, since Zephron had not been with me for this part of the journey.

Even with Aerobellan so reduced in size, climbing down the cliff I'd had to scale when I first made the trip was tricky. Finally we wrapped the horn in my shirt. Zephron climbed down first, using the handholds I showed him. When he was at the bottom, I lay on my stomach, stretched down as far as I could, then dropped the bundle into his waiting hands.

Together we walked to the green sphere. I stared at it with intense desire. On the other side was our world . . . and my mother.

"Ready?" asked Zephron.

I hesitated, then said, "After what happened the last time, I'm nervous about whether you'll make it through."

Zephron nodded. "I can certainly understand that. But with Mokurra gone, this should be fine."

"All right. But for safety's sake, let's hold hands while we go through."

Zephron reached out. I took his hand. Together, we walked forward until we were swallowed in green.

When we stepped into the cavern with its seven glowing spheres I felt a rush of relief. Zephron was still with me!

The relief was immediately followed by fear. Had the time peg worked, too? Had we really returned with no time elapsed at all?

"Let's hurry," I said. "We need to get to the top of the mountain so you can start the winds again."

"Yes, we do," said Zephron.

When we entered the main cave Shamoondra raised her enormous head, gazed at us for a moment as if a bit surprised, then went back to sleep. This simple gesture convinced me that we really had returned just after leaving. The great cat felt no need to greet us with "Where have you been all this time?!" eagerness. As far as she was concerned, we had been gone no longer than the time it took us to walk to the green sphere and back!

We climbed the ramp that led to the top of the mountain. Once there, Zephron placed the horn on the stony surface. Moving counterclockwise, he walked around it three times, chanting strange words that made my ears tingle. The horn began to glow. Then it shook. And then it grew . . .

I helped Zephron return the horn to its proper position in the metal frame. When it was settled in place he put his hands on my shoulders, smiled, and said, "Thank you, Hurricane. Thank you for everything."

Then he slipped inside the coils of horn, placed his lips to the mouthpiece, and played the wind to life.

The notes that emerged from the horn were rich, deep,

and mellow. The music went straight to my heart and I felt tears start in my eyes. Not from sorrow. What I felt now was pure joy.

As the Windlord continued to work the valves and keys, the music picked up speed and became more complex.

A moment later I felt a breeze swirl around us!

My tears came faster now. The wind was back, the wind I had loved all my life, the true wind of my birth. It lifted my heart and with a shout I leaped into the air.

Zephron worked the horn for hours, never repeating the same themes, constantly shifting the keys and valves so that the winds went sailing one way and then another.

How long would it take them to travel around the world . . . to reach Chicago? And when they did reach Chicago, would it be in time for my mother?

The sky grew dark before Zephron finally slipped out of Aerobellan's coils. Voice ragged with exhaustion, he said, "I need to rest. Then we will take you home."

And, all unexpectedly, my heart split in two.

I could not wait to get home. I *ached* to get home. But how could I leave this place, which from the instant I entered it had felt like a second home?

How could I go back to being the boy I used to be, now that I had seen the things I had seen, done the things I had done?

How could I be just a kid again, with five billion souls still jostling for my attention?

My mother, yes . . . she was home, and she was everything to me. Our block, our street, our friends, even the local crazies were part of home, too. But now Zephron was also home. This cave was home, a home that fit like the missing piece into a hole in my heart that had been waiting to be filled.

Zephron put his arm around my shoulder and I supported him as we walked down the ramp, back into the cave.

"That was a week's worth of seeding winds," he muttered. I tried to guide him to his hammock, but he insisted on first going to the opposite wall, where he opened another of those secret niches. "I'm sorry I don't have a bed, or an extra hammock," he said as he pulled out a thick blanket. "I'm not used to having visitors."

"I'll be fine," I said firmly. "Come on, you need to rest."

I steered him back to the hammock. He climbed in and was instantly asleep. I went to the table, sat, ate some of the bread and cheese that never diminished, and gazed at the Windlord for a long time.

Later, clutching the blanket he had given me, I went to the shelf of rock that thrust out at the front of the cave. Sitting at its edge, I dangled my feet over the abyss. Then I wrapped the blanket around me and stared up at the stars, wondering how many billions of worlds there were out there—and what kind of people might live on them.

I don't know how long I had been sitting there when Shamoondra settled in beside me. I relaxed back against her. Though the drop over the edge was thousands of feet,

I didn't worry. I knew the tiger wouldn't let me fall. I fell asleep listening to her purr.

The dreams I dreamed were not my own. They were shaped by memories of a lost world, a world destroyed by the folly of the people who lived there. Yet they were not all nightmares, not all filled with rage and regret. Some were sweet, and sweetly sad, pulsing with yearning for what might have been, and for what had been lost. Amid these flashes of beauty and horror, in a moment of half wakefulness, I realized I had been tossing and turning but was held in place by a great paw that kept me safe from rolling over the edge, into the void.

When I woke in the morning Zephron was sitting close by.

"Good sleep?" he asked.

"Not sure I would go that far," I said, yawning.

"Unfamiliar memories?"

I nodded.

"I suspect a lifetime of that may be the price of having saved the world."

"Have we really saved it? How fast will the winds recover? I know you don't like it when I get all scientific, but I also know that a wind going fifty miles an hour can be pretty destructive. And even at that speed it would take almost a day for it to go a thousand miles . . . which means it will be days and days and days before the winds get back to where my mom is!"

Zephron smiled. "Your thinking is good, as far as it goes. But let me give you another way to consider it. Did you ever stand up a row of dominoes?"

"How do you know about dominoes?"

He waved a hand. "I pay attention to the world I serve. Now do you want to know the good news or not?"

"I want to know!"

"So, I'm assuming you know about standing up a row of dominoes, then pushing one over and watching them topple forward one after another. It's like that now. When I first told you how I create the winds I mentioned seeds. As the winds I started last night move outward they will waken other winds that went dormant when the horn was stolen. Those revived winds will rush forward and wake more winds ahead of them. It will be a waterfall of winds, a cascade of winds. There will indeed be some damage, which I regret. But these are great forces that cannot be completely controlled. Before this day is over the wind will be waking all around the world."

He looked at me and I saw sadness in his eyes.

"What's wrong?" I asked. "I thought you would be happy."

"I am, mostly. But . . . well, do you want to go home now?"

Once more something inside me broke. "I do," I said. "I do so much. I have to. But I don't want to leave this place."

Zephron stood. I ran to his arms. He held me while I wept, my tears flowing into that wild white beard of his.

I'm not sure, but I think the Windlord cried, too.

When we finally pulled apart he said, "If we leave now, we can be in Chicago a few hours past midnight."

The journey home was different from the outward trip. For one thing, we had a good tail wind, since the winds were still moving outward from his cave. And the world . . . well, this is hard to explain, but the world felt *right* in a way it had not before. The clouds were moving, and I saw great patches of open sky above the sea, where before there had been only that endless layer of gray.

Not soon enough, yet all too soon, we emerged from the Enchanted Realm. As we flew over Chicago I could see that Zephron had told the truth. The winds had arrived ahead of us and the air was already cleaner than it had been the night he came to ask me to help him find the horn.

We landed on the roof of the Jerrold Arms. Shamoondra crouched to let us slide down.

"I cannot stay," said Zephron. "There will be many more people out and about now than that night I came to get you. I do not want to be seen—do not want Shamoondra to be seen."

"I understand," I said. Then, with a surge of need and hope and hunger that twisted my heart, I whispered, "Will I ever see you again?"

Zephron closed his eyes. "I don't know. I hope so."

"What does that mean?"

The Windlord shook his head. "Can't talk about it, don't want to jinx it." He reached inside his vest, pulled out a ring, and said, "But there is this."

"What is it?"

"Put it on."

The ring was too big, and I was afraid it would fall right off my finger. But as I slid it on I could feel the size adjusting.

Magic, of course.

"What will it do?" I asked.

"It will let you read the wind, just as you've always wanted. While you wear this ring the wind can tell you where it's been, what it's seen."

I looked at his face, studied his eyes. "There's more, isn't there?"

Zephron smiled. "Yes. When the conditions are right, and the wind is from the east, it will let me send you messages. Not much, just a hello. Just a 'How are you doing?'"

"And will I be able to answer?"

"Yes, when the wind comes from the west. And now . . . I really must leave you, Hurricane." He put his hands on my shoulders and looked directly into my eyes. "You know what you've done. And I know. But we also know that no one else will understand if you try to tell them. Nor will anyone understand the price you will continue to pay, the dreams from other lives that will forever haunt you. You, however, will always know that the world owes you its life. Now, don't wait for morning. Go to your mother."

He embraced me again, then turned and climbed onto Shamoondra. A moment later they were gone, and I stood alone on the top of the Jerrold Arms. Eventually I made my way down to our apartment.

I put on some clean clothes—I couldn't see Mom in the state I was in. Then, feeling almost ready, I walked to the clinic. Hope and terror dogged my every step.

The night nurse looked startled to see me. "Shouldn't you be home in bed?" she asked.

"Couldn't sleep," I replied.

She smiled. "Well, visiting hours are long over and I shouldn't let you in. But as it happens, your mother couldn't sleep, either. She's been asking for you. So why don't you go see her."

I pulled in a deep breath and tried not to let it out as a sob. She was alive!

"Come on," the nurse said gently. "I'll take you to her."

Mom's room was barely a room, the bed little more than a cot. But she was sitting up. When I walked in, her eyes grew wide and she managed to smile and cry at the same time. I flinched as she tried to stand. Quickly the nurse said, "Don't you dare, Mrs. Smith. He's here, and that's all that matters."

I went to her and we threw our arms around each other.

"Hurricane! Oh, Hurricane, I've been so worried about you!"

"You think *you* were worried?" I cried. "I've been scared to death!"

"But where have you been? There were two whole days when no one could find you!"

I looked at her and smiled. Then I said, "Sit back and relax, Mom. It's my turn to tell *you* a story."